MURDER WITH MADNESS

BLYTHE BAKER

~

Sylvia and Miles travel to London to investigate the murder of Miles' late wife. At last, Miles is about to solve the crime that has haunted him for so long. There's just one problem. The killer is dangerous and cunning.

With Miles tracking down leads in the city, can Sylvia uncover the truth during a deadly weekend in the English countryside? Or will the killer strike again one final, terrible time?

~

1

————

"I cannot remember the last time I had such an enjoyable train ride," I said. "I must admit I am rather disappointed that it is coming to an end so soon."

Miles smiled at me from the other side of the compartment. It had taken me some time to get used to seeing him in what I realized must have been the typical attire of his previous life; suits of fine wool, ties of silk, derby or bowler hats with pristine ribbons. He truly looked a man of stature, now that he was no longer dressed like the rest of our household staff.

"I confess I never thought I would take a train from Southampton to London ever again," he said. "Though I wish I took as much pleasure in the trip as you do."

I glanced out the window at the passing country-side. I needed to remind myself that this was not a holiday, much as it might seem to be to those on the outside. "I have not yet forgotten that we have come with a job to do," I said. "By the time we return to New York, you will be a free man once more."

Miles nodded, but turned away to gaze out the window himself.

An uneasy feeling washed over me, one that I had been feeling since we had first concocted our scheme to come to London almost three weeks ago. It came every time we discussed what would happen after we were finished with looking into his late wife's murder. Whenever I mentioned the both of us returning to New York, Miles seemed to grow quiet. Not for the first time, I wondered if he had no intention of joining me for the return journey.

"I am pleased our plan worked out as smoothly as it did," Miles said. "That your friend was as willing to house us as she was."

"As am I," I said. "I realize that it is only a short time before her wedding, but she could not have been more pleased that I had written to her, asking to visit. When I explained that you were hoping to visit some family in the city, she was relieved that I would not be traveling to her alone."

"And you did not tell her our real intentions," he said.

I shook my head. "No, as I said a few nights ago, all she knows is that I am coming to visit her, and she has graciously extended the invitation for you to stay as well."

He nodded. "Very good," he said. "I imagine she will suspect nothing if I leave to go and investigate throughout the city."

"She will think nothing of me wanting to explore as well," I said.

He frowned. "Miss Sylvia...I have been trying to decide how to say this, but I think it would be best if I pursued this matter on my own."

I stared at him. "Miles, I thought this was the entire point of my accompanying you?"

He looked down at his hands folded together in his lap. The tension on his face told me he struggled with his next words. "At first, I agreed. You are very clever at working out complicated mysteries, Miss Sylvia, but I worry that this will put you in grave danger. I cannot risk that. Your parents think I have accompanied you on a holiday, not a murder investigation."

My brow furrowed. Did this mean all I could contribute would be a place for him to stay while we were in London? "I thought you said the police in London were after you," I said. "Will they not recognize you? Or will not someone else in the city recognize you?"

"I will have to do most of my investigating after dark," he said. "Avoiding familiar places, and – "

"Would it not be more advantageous for someone

like me, whom no one will recognize, to go out and do some searching?" I asked. "I would be able to move around the city entirely beneath the nose of the police, and they would be none the wiser."

Miles frowned. "Perhaps it is time I told you that I am now almost entirely convinced that I know who did this," he said.

"I thought you had your suspicions," I said. "But how did you find out for certain?"

"It has been the same man I have suspected all along, the only man with any real reason to have tried to harm me," he said. "Not to mention that he would have been able to convincingly portray me that night in the park."

"What do you mean?" I asked. "Do you have a brother?"

"A brother?" he asked. "No, I do not have a brother. I have sisters, all of whom are younger than I. No, I believe it is a cousin of mine...a cousin who would ultimately inherit my share of our family's property and wealth if I were to die without an heir."

My eyes widened. "My word, that does seem like the sort of reason someone would be driven to murder," I said. "Why did you say nothing before?"

Miles swallowed hard. "He...he was a dear friend of mine growing up. It was not until I believe he realized that his inheritance from his own family would be far less substantial than what I would stand to inherit, that he...changed."

"Was he not to be well off?" I asked.

"No, he most certainly was," he said. "But you see, my family and whatever children I had would not only have our home in London, but the estate out in the countryside where my father has his stables. We would have the business, and be guaranteed to live very well off it. He would inherit his family's home just outside of London, and not a great deal more. Not unless...I were to die without offspring. In that case, after the deaths of my parents, all that should have come to me might instead go to the next male living relation—my uncle and, through him, my cousin himself."

"Then his attitude came down to nothing more than greed," I said. "And envy."

"That is my suspicion," Miles said. "I have no proof, though. That is the trouble that I have run into for the last several months. I have been trying to find some proof, some letter, some recollection of an encounter that would have proven that anything had gone awry."

"You told me you suspected he had fled to New York," I said. "Why?"

"Well...his father owns a shipping business," he said. "That is how he made his wealth, whereas mine has been passed through the family. I caught wind that my cousin had gone to New York to inspect a new shipping yard his father was having built, but I am quite certain that it was nothing more than a means of not only avoiding official questioning, but maybe an opportunity of destroying evidence."

"Evidence?" I asked. "Such as your pistol?"

Miles patted his hip absently. I had made sure to return the weapon to him before we left New York. "No, he could have discarded that anywhere," he said. "As it was, he left it at my house in London, and I took it with me before I left. It was not until I reached New York and began looking into things that I suspected he must have used this gun, and as such, I needed to dispose of it."

"What sort of evidence, then?" I asked.

"Perhaps he wrote something down, or took something of Sophia's after killing her," Miles said. "Even if he didn't, at the very least, he may have talked to someone in New York or back in London. I have a hard time believing my cousin came to the decision to take Sophia's life on a whim. Therefore, there had to have been planning that went into it. Planning could mean collaboration, though I have yet to find anyone who has direct connections with him in regards to the murder..." He shook his head. "He was thorough. He had to make sure that I would not be at home, and that the staff at my house would not see him enter the house or leave, a feat that I have yet to understand."

"Still, there is a strong likelihood that he has left

some evidence somewhere," I said. "Yet you have not been able to find it."

"Precisely," he said. "The benefit of being in London is that I will be able to find ways to get nearer to him, perhaps even to those he is closest with."

"Will they not recognize you?" I asked.

"That is what I am uncertain of," Miles said. "Most people must know that I fled the city, or perhaps they believe I was caught. Regardless, I doubt I shall be at the forefront of the minds of those close to him... unless they had an involvement in the murder, as well."

"It is certainly possible," I said. "There could have been accomplices."

Miles sighed, leaning back against the seat in the train car. For a while, the only sound between us was the *click-clacking* of the tracks beneath us.

"It does make a great deal of sense..." I said. "He went after your wife as a means of preventing you from having any heirs of your own. The pair of you were not married long, were you?"

Miles shook his head. "No, not long. And perhaps, given the situation, it is for the best that there were no children yet..."

I frowned. I did not wish to sadden him any further by speaking of his late wife. "Without children, then you said your cousin is to ultimately inherit your fortunes when you pass," I said. "And I assume that if he managed to successfully frame you for the murder, and the police caught you, there would be little chance of you ever getting out of prison."

"I would be hanged," Miles said, his voice empty of emotion.

"And now your cousin is back in London," I said. "Why?"

"I assume his work in New York was complete," Miles said. "That, or he believed that enough time had passed since the murder that he could return without suspicion. If I had not fled when I did, I have little doubt his plan would have been completed."

The thought was indeed troubling. How many murders like this one occurred, with those responsible never caught or brought to justice?

"What I still do not understand is why you wish to tackle this problem yourself," I said. "I realize full well that you are worried about me being in danger, but it would be far better for us both if we worked together."

"You do not understand what you suggest," Miles said. "If we were caught, then you would be charged with aiding a known criminal. It would not matter what I said, I would be seen as guilty and, if you were with me, so would you be."

"I realize the circumstances are more difficult than those we typically work under," I said. "But we have solved crimes together before."

"This one is different," he said, his expression stern.

"The police may not be looking for me right now, but if anyone sees me, if anyone recognizes me, they could hurry off to the authorities and it will be all over for me."

"Yes, I understand all that," I said. "Which is why you would be wise to develop a disguise...and we should play the part together, make it all the more believable."

He frowned. "What do you mean?" he asked.

"Well..." I said. "What if we played the same couple that we once played when we were investigating a crime at the horse races?" Suddenly, I perked up. "Wait – it only just occurs to me. You were so incredibly knowledgeable during that investigation, and told me that you spent a great deal of time in the stables. You were not lying to me."

"Did you think I was?" he asked.

"No..." I said. "I suppose I just never expected it to be because you were the son of an owner, and not one of the stable boys there for work."

He smirked at me. "You are suggesting we should portray the same young couple that we did at the races?"

"It fooled everyone there, did it not?" I asked. "Though perhaps instead of being already married, we could simply be engaged. People will think nothing of a lovesick young couple, will they?"

Miles scratched the side of his face. "It does seem

as if people tend to ignore those sorts, don't they?"

"Precisely," I said. "Which is why I believe this plan will work."

He sighed rather heavily. "Miss Sylvia, I do worry that this is unwise..." he said. "If your father knew the real reason why I wished to return to London, he would never let me set foot in your household ever again."

"I realize that," I said. "Which is precisely why you need my help. The faster we can address this, the faster we can clear your name."

"It is going to take something irrefutable," he said. "I know full well that the killer will never admit to it. He would rather take the truth with him to the grave."

"Is he that sort?" I asked. "Unable to be coerced?"

"No," Miles said. "He is a strong man, with strong convictions. Unfortunately, they always seem to be for the wrong reasons and the wrong people. He has always thought very highly of himself, but I never thought him capable of going to these extremes..."

"Well...you have some time to consider my offer," I said. "I do hope you realize that I am here for you, and wish to help you."

"I do," he said, his tone gentle. "And I thank you for it."

The population grew denser as we drew nearer to the city. The lush, rolling fields gave way to charming little neighborhoods and soon to stretches of river and long, packed streets. London, it seemed, had changed since I had seen her last.

I stole a glance at Miles out of the corner of my eye. His face, set in a determined expression, stared intently out the window at the city that had betrayed him so thoroughly...the city where his wife had been stolen from him.

I pitied him and wondered just how miserable he must have been in our home, when he finally retired in the evenings to his room, all alone, living a life that was nothing more than a lie. How it must have pained him to be reduced to acting as a mere butler, waiting on my family when he may well have been brought up in a higher place in society than any of us.

*It is wrong...*I thought. *If he does choose to come back to New York with me, then I shall have my father assist him in acquiring a more fitting position. It will never make up for what he lost, but he will not return with me to serve as our butler any longer. He will be the man that he should be, and be presented as he truly is.*

Ever since that night in the parlor, wherein Miles finally confessed the truth to me, I realized my perception of him had changed entirely. I had always respected him, come to rely on him, and trusted him. But it was as if learning about his life in London, about his wife, his home, had made him a fuller person to me. And in a way, he was a stranger to me all over again.

"Are you all right, Miss Sylvia?"

I blinked, looking up at him. I had not realized I had been staring at him. "Oh – Yes, of course. I'm sorry. I suppose this is all a great deal to take in, and I am simply reflecting on it all."

He gave me a more reserved smile. "I truly cannot thank you enough for being so willing to help me. I am in your debt."

I shook my head. "That is where you are wrong. You have saved my life more than once, and this is the least I can do to repay you for that."

He did not argue. "Let us just hope we won't need to be in such dangerous situations again."

The train whistle blew, and I could feel the cars begin to slow.

"And Miss Sylvia…" Miles said, getting to his feet to fetch the suitcases from the rack near the door. "I do hope you will find the means by which to enjoy yourself on this trip."

I straightened. "Well…it has been some time since I was here, and since I last saw my friend. I certainly hope there will be some time for fun. I hope the same for you, too."

He smiled, but I saw little joy in his gaze. "I have too much to think about for the time being. If we manage to…to resolve this matter…then I shall be able to have true joy and peace for the first time since I last saw my Sophia."

His words hung heavy in the compartment.

Soon, we were greeted by one of the engineers, and helped off the train. King's Cross was bustling as it always was whenever I had been there before. My heart leapt with excitement as we made our way to the platform. My friend Elizabeth had written to let me know that the day we arrived, she would be sending someone from her house to come and get us.

What I had not expected was that she would send her fiancé.

I had met the man during one of my prior trips to London, and he seemed as cheery as I remembered. Handsome and tall, he had hair the color of honey, and rosy cheeks. He wore a bowler hat of sapphire blue, and held a handsome sign written in a neat calligraphy. He recognized me just as we approached, giving us a friendly wave.

"Miss Shipman! How wonderful it is to see you!"

"Mr. Walton," I said, beaming at him. "My, it is lovely to see you, as well."

"And this must be your friend," Mr. Walton said, turning to Miles. "How do you do?"

"Well, sir, thank you," Miles said, shaking his hand.

Mr. Walton brightened even more. "Ah, a Londoner!" he exclaimed. "What a surprise!"

"That I am," Miles said. "Born in Gloucestershire, spent a great deal of my life in London."

"Well then, may I be the first to welcome you

home?" he asked. He folded up the sign and tucked it beneath his arm.

"That could only have been done by your lovely fiancé," I said with a grin.

"I suppose you would know, being schoolfellows as you were," Mr. Walton said. "Come, she will never forgive me if I delay in getting you home to her."

I turned to look at Miles, and to my great delight, I saw him grinning. It might have been the fact that he was back in London. It might have been because he finally had the chance to see his home once again. Regardless, it seemed that my assessment had been right that this trip could be the best thing for him.

As we followed Mr. Walton out, hearing some exuberant commentary from the man, I found myself filled with a renewed determination to assist Miles. I *would* help him to find his cousin, and I *would* help him to find the irrefutable proof that he needed in order to prove his innocence. I had the experience. I had done this sort of thing before. It would take all of my wits... but if I was honest with myself, I *wanted* to do this.

I chanced another glance at Miles. Now that I knew the truth and all my uneasy suspicions about him were gone, I could count him as my friend, and fully jump into this with my whole heart. There was no longer a need to avoid him. There was no need to question him. All I wanted was for him to have the closure that he so deserved.

2

"Oh, you're here, you're here! You're finally here!"

It amazed me that I had not seen Elizabeth for years now, yet at the sound of her voice, and the familiarity of it, it was as if no time had passed. I staggered under her embrace as she flung herself into my arms just as soon as I crossed the threshold of her family's charming London home, a home that would soon be hers and her new husband's once they were married in a few weeks' time. A gift from her parents, I was told, in addition to the land and estate he would inherit in Bath.

I grinned into her bouncing, pale blonde curls as she nearly squeezed the very air from my lungs. "How I have missed you, my friend."

She squealed as she gave me one last squeeze. She

leaned away, bright eyed and pink in the cheeks. "Sylvia, you look so well! You have really become a lovely woman in my absence!"

"You say it as if your leaving had something to do with it," I teased her.

She giggled. "Oh, how can you be so unkind?" she said. "You have the expression of a woman in love, you do."

"I thought the same, my dear," Mr. Walton said with a grin as he stepped out of the way as their butler carried our suitcases over the threshold of the front door. "She has that radiant glow."

I flushed scarlet, shaking my head. "You are mistaken, my friend," I said.

Elizabeth frowned at me, seeming to droop. "But the last I knew, you had gone to visit your aunt in order to 'meet new people'. Was it not a successful trip?"

"Successful may not be the word that I would choose..." I said.

"Well, that is a shame," she said. She brightened again, though, as she turned to Miles. "And this must be your friend. Mr. Miles, was it?"

He smiled graciously at her. "How do you do?"

Her eyes flew open wider at his accent. "Oh! Sylvie didn't tell me you were from London!"

"That I am," he said.

"Isn't it interesting, darling?" Mr. Walton said,

coming to stand with us. "I was surprised to learn it as well."

"I must say that I am not familiar with the surname Miles, though," Elizabeth said, her brow furrowing.

"This is a big city," Miles said. "I imagine that our families must run in different circles."

"Quite possible," Mr. Walton said, without any trace of irony.

To my relief, neither Elizabeth nor her fiancé made any reference to Miles being a butler, both welcoming him as easily as if he were a guest of equal status. Perhaps my last letter to Elizabeth had made it clear that he traveled with me as more of a companion than a servant. Then again, I recalled that Elizabeth had never been one for snobbery anyway.

"Oh, Sylvia, how rude of me," Elizabeth said suddenly. "Come along, you must be famished after your long trip. Please, come in and have something to eat."

She led us through the handsome foyer and in through a short hall where a pair of double doors greeted us. Mr. Walton pushed them open and beyond lay the sort of parlor that I adored; comfortable furnishings, polished wooden shelves filled with leather-bound books, and a bay window that over-looked the tree-lined street.

"Have a seat wherever you like," Elizabeth said.

Miles followed close behind me, and pulled out a

chair near the fire for me. "I suppose I should not be all together surprised to find the old city raining once again."

Mr. Walton chuckled as he pulled a handkerchief from his front pocket, along with a small pair of spectacles. "As consistent as the sun itself, the weather in this city is," he said. "I have yet to see the sun in my life."

Elizabeth gave her fiancé a chiding smile before reaching between our chairs to take my hand in her own. "How was your trip? Was the weather across the ocean all right?"

"It was better than I expected," I said. "And uneventful, which I am thankful for."

"Apart from that rather raucous snoring from the room beside mine," Miles said.

I shot him a look. "You mean the room that you insisted I switch?" I asked.

"For that precise reason," Miles said. "There was no sound reason why you should have to suffer through it instead of me."

"But you hardly caught any sleep apart from the few hours you rested in the middle of the afternoons," I said.

"I made the most of it," he said with a shrug.

I smirked at him, and he returned it easily. He had been insistent that we trade cabins aboard the ship. "To be honest, I feared that he thought the man in the neighboring cabin might be dangerous," I said. "And he wanted to make sure that I was protected."

Miles arched a brow. "You never told me that," he said.

"I thought you were merely using the snoring as an excuse," I said. "It isn't as if it would be entirely out of the question, would it?"

Mr. Walton took a seat on the settee near Elizabeth, his brow furrowing. "Do you often run into dangerous men?" he asked.

Elizabeth turned her gaze to him, her eyes growing wide. "Oh, dear, I suppose I never told you, did I?" she asked. "My dear friend has taken up sleuthing, like a detective in a novel."

"Is that so?" Mr. Walton asked, leaning on the arm of Elizabeth's chair. "My word, how unusual. Not to mention frightening."

"That is precisely what I thought," Elizabeth said. She nodded fervently. "I suppose I thought it best to wait to bring such things up, but I have been dying to ask you about all this investigation business. How in the world did you get started doing that?"

I glanced at Miles, who gave me an uncertain shrug. *As long as I am careful to avoid discussing the real reason for our visit, then I think it would be safe to share,* I thought. *My whole family knows, so why should a friend who I have known for many, many years not know?*

"Well...I suppose it started when my uncle died last

October," I said. "He...fell from several stories high, and perished."

"You poor dear..." Elizabeth said with a frown. "I had no idea."

"Something seemed terribly suspicious about the whole affair, especially since many people thought he took his own life. It did not sit right with me, and while everyone else in my family wanted to move on, I was not satisfied with what everyone was thinking. I just could not accept the idea that my uncle would have taken his own life. It did not seem believable."

"Well, not only that, but your father was quite preoccupied at the time with the stock market crash," Miles said.

I nodded. "Which played into the death far more than I might have realized at the time," I said. "After some time, and a great deal of snooping around, I managed to discover who it was that killed my uncle."

"You uncovered the truth all by yourself?" Elizabeth asked.

"Well, not entirely alone," I said. I gestured over my shoulder to Miles. "Miles has quite the eye for these sorts of things, and was quick to offer his help. Without his involvement, I likely never would have found the truth."

Elizabeth gazed back and forth between the both of us. "My goodness, what a pair you are," she said, mystified.

"What happened?" Mr. Walton asked. "When the culprit was found?"

I pursed my lips, looking down at my hands in my lap. "He...well, when I went to confront him, he tried to attack me. After a scuffle, he fell himself, and he...well, I do not know when or how, precisely, but he died, too."

"Indeed?" Mr. Walton asked, shaking his head.

"You put yourself in harm's way?" Elizabeth asked. "So effortlessly?"

"I certainly did not try to," I said. "But I knew something happened to my uncle, and I did not want his death to go by without knowing the truth."

"But you wrote me that delving into such crimes has become a regular interest for you now," Elizabeth went on. "Can I assume that you have taken on more than just that one case?"

I nodded. "Indeed. I believe I have solved..." I counted on my fingers. "Five murders. Well, four, I suppose. One kidnapping that could have turned out for the worse."

Mr. Walton looked as if his eyes might take leave of his head. "My word..." he said.

"How fascinating," Elizabeth said. "And you have been successful?"

"I have been," I said.

She shook her head. "And you wrote that you did it because you wished to help people," she said. She glanced over at Mr. Walton. "Goodness, if only someone we knew was in need of such services. I would be glad to recommend you, as you seem to have such great success."

I laughed. "Oh, no, that's perfectly all right," I said. "I certainly don't wish misfortune on anyone merely so I can solve the crime."

"Miss Sylvia was quite clear that this trip was a means of having a bit of a break from such endeavors," Miles said at the same time.

"My focus while I am here shall be you," I said, smiling at Elizabeth. "That is the whole reason why I came. It has been so long since we have seen one another, and I should like to leave the investigations alone for the time being."

She grinned at me. "Oh, Sylvie...I am so glad that you have come."

I returned her smile, though guilt squirmed in my stomach. That had been almost entirely a lie. Miles and I had needed a place to stay so that we might look into his wife's murder, and I knew that Elizabeth would say yes without question. I did indeed hope to help plan the wedding, help her in any way I could, but our real reason for being here was the investigation.

"This does make me wonder, though," Elizabeth said, scratching her chin. "When you wrote to me a short time ago, before asking to come out here to visit, you were looking into another investigation. It surprised me, as it was about something that happened here."

Miles stiffened behind me, and I cleared my throat.

Of all the cases she could have asked me about...

It made sense, really. She was correct that I had sent a letter to her with the purpose of asking after Miles' wife's murder. At the time, my suspicion had been squarely pointed at Miles, but we had since had our conversation in which he absolved himself. I had not considered what to do or say if she asked me about it again.

"Yes, it was one that I had heard about myself," I said. "At the time, I thought it might help a case that I was looking into." Not a complete lie, but certainly misleading. I had been investigating Miles without his knowledge, and therefore it was a case...in a way.

"I suppose it would have taken its time to make its way across the Atlantic," Elizabeth said.

"Which investigation did you mean, darling?" Mr. Walton asked.

Oh really, now, we do not need to discuss this any further, I thought. *Miles may very well keel over if we keep dancing around the topic.*

"The one about that wealthy young lady murdered in Hyde Park," Elizabeth said. "Sylvie had asked about it in a recent letter."

Mr. Walton shook his head. "What a tragedy. The whole city talked of it."

I chanced a glance at Miles who shifted his weight on his feet behind me. I had to force my expression to remain as smooth as possible, as I found him looking rather curious. When he caught me watching him, he gave me a questioning, encouraging look. *Does he really wish for me to continue?* "Was she well known?" I asked.

"I imagine she was, given her husband's position," said Mr. Walton. "And her family, I believe, is in the precious metals business."

Once again, I resisted the urge to look over at Miles. "I believe I heard about this myself," Miles said. "Friends in the area here and all that. What happened again, precisely?"

Clever, trying to get an outsider's perspective, I thought.

"A young lady went walking with her husband through Hyde Park one evening, and out of nowhere, he attacked her. Shot her, point blank, boom, dead," Mr. Walton said, shaking his head. "It was witnessed by almost ten people, as the hour was not terribly late. Murders in a city of this size are not unusual, as you can imagine, but the details of this one excited quite a bit of attention from the press."

"What happened next?" I asked. "Did he flee?"

Elizabeth nodded. "He took off without looking back, we have heard," she said.

"I heard that someone tried to chase him down,

too," Mr. Walton said. "To no avail, it seems. He managed to escape."

"To where?" Miles asked. "How could someone so dastardly hide so successfully?"

"That is the question, isn't it?" asked Mr. Walton. "How could he hide?"

"No one has any idea," Elizabeth said. "I am quite certain that it would have been all over the papers if they had ever managed to catch him."

Miles nodded. "I certainly hope they do catch him," he said.

"As do I," I said. "That poor woman deserves to have her killer found."

"But why her husband, though?" Mr. Walton asked. "How could he have chosen to kill her so easily?"

"How could anyone choose to kill so easily?" Elizabeth asked.

"If I have learned anything from the investigations I have taken part in, it is that often these things are not as they seem," I said. I felt Miles' eyes on the back of my head, and knew that might sound too cryptic. "What I mean is that those who commit these horrible acts are often close to those who died, but I have been genuinely surprised to find that the guilty party does not always end up being who I thought it was. Even so, it has frequently been someone that I never thought could do something so horrendous to someone they claimed to love deeply."

"How awful..." Elizabeth said.

"She is right," Miles said. "It isn't only that those nearest to the victim generally have the greatest chance of committing the crime. They are the people closest to them emotionally, and often, those emotions can become quite strong."

*Speaking from experience...*I thought. *Multiple experiences, even.*

"Did you by any chance know the victim?" I asked Elizabeth. "You speak of the situation as if you knew her."

"Oh, my family did not," Elizabeth said. She looked over at Mr. Walton. "But Mr. Walton's family lives just a few blocks away from their home."

My cheeks burned. *Of all the places...*

"Yes, and it is quite intriguing because there has been some activity in that house as of late," Mr. Walton said. "After it has sat empty for almost a year now, yes?"

"Perhaps not quite so long," Elizabeth said. "But I assume it must be the family coming to take ownership of the estate, even if the authorities have yet to find who committed the murder."

"Likely to go to whomever was meant to inherit it..." Miles said, a slight edge to his words. "As I wonder if there was an heir, it will most likely go to the next member of the family."

"Oh, if they did have a child, imagine how young it would be," Elizabeth said with yet another frown.

"Far too young to take possession of the home," Mr. Walton said. "If they did not have any children, then it might be passed to a brother."

"If any brother existed," Miles said.

Mr. Walton nodded in agreement.

"Well, maybe it will be the first steps of putting that tragedy behind the city," Elizabeth said. "Time continues to pass, even if there are those evils that manage to succeed in this world."

"It's true..." I said.

The door to the parlor opened, and the family butler strode inside. "Miss Elizabeth, and esteemed guests...dinner is served."

I was grateful for the chance to move away from the subject of Miles' wife and her death. I could only imagine his feelings on the news of people moving around in the house. *He will think it is his cousin preparing to take the house. This will surely spur him on.*

The dining room had been decorated with garlands of ivy above the windows, and two matching silver candelabras standing bright and shimmering on the center of the table.

"Elizabeth, this is not all for us, is it?" I asked as Miles helped me into my designated chair.

She grinned. "Well, I saw no trouble in putting up some decorations early for you to enjoy," she said with a laugh. "I would have wanted to shower you with affection, of course, but there is another reason for all this."

Mr. Walton took a seat at the table across from me, and gestured to the chair beside him. "Mr. Miles, are you coming to join us?"

Miles glanced at me; it seemed as if they were not quite sure how to treat him after all.

"Oh, come now," Elizabeth said. "You are here on a holiday, are you not? To visit with family?"

"Well, yes," Miles said.

"Then you need not bother yourself with your usual routine," she said. "We have our staff here. While you are visiting, you are our guest, and we are very happy to have you."

"Well...thank you," Miles said, and went to join Mr. Walton on the opposite side of the table.

He gave me a bit of a shy grin, and I returned it. *This is how it should be, given his family's wealth. Once his name is cleared, he will no longer need to hide like this right out in the open. He will be able to be who he was meant to be.*

Elizabeth gave us a firm nod. "Very good. Now, as I was saying, these decorations were a bit of a trial to see if I liked them or not."

"For the wedding?" I asked.

"Yes," Elizabeth said. "But also for decorating for the party we are having tomorrow evening."

"A party?" I asked.

Elizabeth beamed at her fiancé, and he returned it just as warmly. "Peter has not yet been introduced to some of my extended family, and my parents thought it appropriate to have a dinner in which we might make full introductions. Of course, you both are invited."

"How wonderful," I said, smiling at her. "We would be happy to be present. And if you are in need of any help preparing for the party, of course, we would love to be of service."

Elizabeth clapped her hands together. "Oh, thank you, my friend. I would be thrilled to have your help."

"This is perhaps one of the last social engagements that we have lined up before the wedding," Mr. Walton said. "I am greatly looking forward to meeting the rest of the family. I can only hope that they will approve of me."

"Oh, Peter, if my uncle Fredrick approved of you, then you have nothing to fear," Elizabeth said.

I glanced at Miles, who wore an uneasy smile. *Oh... what if any of the guests recognize him?* I realized. *That would not bode well for our investigation.*

We might very well have to reconsider what we did in terms of helping with wedding events. We only had two weeks here in London, and we would have to make the best use of our time that we could.

"What will you need from me?" I asked. "Shall I help you hang more of these lovely garlands tomorrow?"

"Yes, that would be wonderful," Elizabeth said. "The party starts at six sharp tomorrow evening, with dinner served by eight. I shall need to make sure that the flower arrangements are done by noon, and then the table set by three. Oh, dearest, you are to retrieve your suit by two, yes? And what of the caterers?"

"I believe they said they would be here by ten o'clock," Mr. Walton said.

"Very good," Elizabeth said. She sighed happily. "It always does bring me joy for everything to come together just so."

"Indeed," I said. "And where are your parents this evening?"

"Oh, they are visiting some friends," Elizabeth said. "They will be home later this evening, though, and will be so very happy to see you again."

"And I look forward to seeing them, as well."

I can only hope that her parents will not see Miles and place him immediately. If only I had realized just how difficult this all could be, all the possible people that would know his real identity.

The sooner we could clear his name, the better. Otherwise, I would have to spend the entire two weeks watching that worried, furrowing wrinkle between his brows as we hoped and prayed that we found a lead.

It seemed that it might be time to take a more proactive approach.

3

I stifled a yawn, taking a quick look at the clock on my bedside table. In the gentle light of the lamp beside it, I noticed that it was nearing eleven. My eyes watered as I yawned again, and laid the silk ribbon I had been using for a bookmark into the binding and closed my book.

I rolled over on my bed and set the book down on the table, and sighed.

It had been a pleasant evening with Elizabeth and Mr. Walton, with stories and laughter and a few rounds of Mr. Walton's favorite card game called Seeker. I had never heard of it, but it seemed Miles was familiar with it, as well, which surprised both Mr. Walton and Elizabeth. He said that it was not uncommon for the butlers or other household staff to play the game, as well, but I could see the regret on his face after so openly admitting something that might connect him with the upper class.

*This trip may very well end up being more difficult than I had anticipated...*I thought, glancing toward the door. Miles had walked with me to my room, but had not lingered. We did not have a chance to speak just the two of us, and not for the first time since retiring did I wonder if it would be wise to go and see him. I could not imagine a chance where I might get to speak with him the following morning, getting ready for the dinner party as I had promised Elizabeth I would, and that only left this evening.

I dug through my suitcase until I found my dressing gown and slipped it over my shoulders. The house, as warm as it was, still boasted cold floors against my bare feet. I found my boots and pulled those on. Satisfied that I was dressed as properly as I could be, I stepped out into the dark hall.

The house had fallen asleep already; gentle snores could be heard further down the hall, and apart from the crack beneath Miles' door, I could see no streaks of light peeking out from any room.

I kept to the long, plush rug that ran the length of the hall until I reached Miles' door, not wishing to wake those who were so peacefully resting. I hesitated for only a moment before I realized that I was being foolish. I had come to speak with Miles, the butler...but all I could see now was Miles in his rightful role. He may very well have a higher stature than even my father, yet we had been treating him like a lowly servant. I knew that my family had not mistreated him, and that he could have easily turned the offer of the job down had he wished it when I had offered it to him...but I still found that I could not quite look at him the same way that I used to. Had I ever made him look at me with contempt? Had he ever had to bite his tongue so that he might not turn around and put me in my place?

No, Miles is not that sort of man. He subjected himself to that sort of life, and that is the sort of life to which he fully dedicated himself.

I knocked on the door, and rustling greeted me from the other side. A moment later the door popped open, Miles' green eyes shining in the dark. "Oh, Miss Sylvia..." he said. "Is everything all right?"

"Yes," I said. "I simply wished to speak with you for a few moments without...prying ears."

Miles took a quick look over his shoulder before widening the opening. "Of course, come in," he said.

I slipped inside, and he made sure to close the door behind me with little more than a gentle creak.

He strode over to the bench seat beneath the window where his suitcase lay open, and began to dig through it like a groundhog in a garden.

"You hardly look ready for bed," I said, eyeing the

pressed suit he still wore, along with the traveling
cloak draped over the foot of the bed.

"That's because I am not," he said, finally locating a
hat and giving it a good shake to right the shape. "Far
from it."

My brow furrowed. "Are you going somewhere at
this hour?"

"Well..." Miles said, and then he sighed. "I hardly
have time to waste, do I?"

A chill swept over me as if he'd opened the
window, sending shivers down my arms and legs. "You
are going to your old house, aren't you?"

Miles said nothing, but his mouth formed a thin
line as he set aside a few pairs of socks, still perusing
for something.

"Miles, do you not think that is terribly unwise?" I
asked, my heart jumping at the idea of him getting
caught after all this time. "Of all the places where you
might be recognized, would it not be there?"

"I am not planning to go into the house," he said.
"Especially if it is occupied."

I frowned. "And what are you going to do if it is
occupied?"

He looked down at the socks he held, turning them
over in his hands. "There is nothing I can do, at least
not at the moment. If I am able to clear my name, then
my cousin will not be able to keep that house in the

first place. The inheritance to him will be voided, as my father will surely return it to me."

"I have no doubt," I said. "What do you plan to do when you get there?"

"I don't know," he said. "I suppose I just want to see what is happening, perhaps catch a glimpse of someone from my cousin's household. Anything that I might be able to use against him when the time finally comes."

"Would that really be enough to prove anything?" I asked. "How does that tie him to the murder?"

"It doesn't," Miles said, and I could sense a bit of frustration in his tone. "But it might help me figure out some of his plans."

"Right..." I said. It really did not make a great deal of sense to me what he was thinking, or how that might lead him to the clues that he needed.

"I realize there may only be answers on his person or among his personal affects," Miles said. "Which is going to make this all the more difficult."

"Would he have left anything in your house?" I asked. "If he is moving in, that is."

Miles shook his head. "I cannot imagine he would be foolish enough to do so," he said. "He will have covered his tracks well, and paid off those he needed to in order to keep them quiet."

"So what can we do?" I asked. "If he has been as thorough as that."

"All hope is not lost," he said. "Aha, here you are." He pulled out the pair of socks he had been searching for, having discovered them tucked inside the sleeve of one of his nightshirts. He wandered to the end of the bed and sat upon it to tug the socks on. "You have seen cases where you felt as if you had no evidence, yet you persisted, yes?"

"I suppose," I said. "But will this not require speaking to those closest to your cousin? Or perhaps looking through his things for evidence? Which is why I wondered if you planned on sneaking into your own house for said evidence."

"I don't believe he would be foolish enough to leave something around that would condemn him," he said.

"What about your pistol?" I asked. "I meant to ask how you managed to find it again. Where had he left it?"

Miles smirked. "It is interesting that you mention that, as he did leave it at my house. He thought it would be yet another piece of evidence tying me to the murder. Anyone who knew me would have known the pistol that I favored. As such, when I had a brief moment to sneak into the house before I fled to New York, I grabbed the pistol and brought it with me. Later, I reconsidered, knowing the evidence was far too strong and would horrendously heap guilt upon me. I needed to be rid of it."

I glanced at his writing desk, where his pistol lay in

its holster out in the open. "Yet you seem to have little care that it has returned to you," I said. "Do you not worry that someone will recognize it, and therefore you?"

"They may..." he said, walking over to the desk to retrieve the weapon. "But it has done me far better to remain by my side." With a practiced motion, he slid the holster into his belt.

I smiled. "That's good."

"I am grateful that you found it...even if you thought it tied me to the murder."

"I suppose your cousin did a better job leaving planted clues behind than we realized, if even I suspected you," I said.

His own smirk faded, replaced by a grimace. "Yes, well...that is the mountain that we are up against, isn't it?"

He got to his feet and reached for the traveling cloak. He tossed it over his shoulder, and started toward the door.

"Miles, perhaps I should come with you," I said.

He stopped, giving me a pointed look over his shoulder. "I do not think that would be wise," he said.

"And why not?" I asked. "You have accompanied me on many of my investigations. Would it not be best to have a second set of eyes so that you might see more?"

He smirked. "You really have changed quite a bit, Miss Sylvia."

My mouth fell open. "What do you mean? What does that have to do with any of this?"

He tilted his head, his gaze reminding me of the piercing eyes of an owl perched in a tree. "You have always been a woman of strength, but ever since Joan was kidnapped, you have gained decisiveness as well."

I could not decide what to say to that.

"It is a good thing," he said. "I think it will be difficult for someone to dissuade or take advantage of you."

He walked to the door and pulled it open.

"Wait," I said, stopping him before he could step out alone. "As you say, I am not easily deterred when my mind is made up. I will accompany you."

"Are you sure?" he asked. "The streets can be dangerous at night."

"Of course," I said. "The whole reason we came to London together was to clear your name. Allow me to use my experiences to give you the best chance possible."

He considered the words with a gentle bob of his head.

"We have so little help as it is," I said. "And with our limited time here in town, we need to take advantage of as much as we can."

"All right," he said. "You have made your point, and I see the wisdom in it. Let it be known, though, that I would prefer for you to remain here and allow me to do the dangerous parts. With every other case, we have not been certain of the person who did the murdering. With this...I know it was my cousin. I know what he is capable of, and I fear that he would go to any lengths to ensure the protection of his identity."

"I understand," I said. "And I will be careful, of course."

"You realize that the moment he connects the two of us, it will put you in harm's way," he said.

"I do," I said. "And I am fully prepared to accept that danger."

He nodded. "Very well, then."

"Give me just a few moments to change," I said. I hurried down the hall to my own room once again, and changed into something better to go out in. I chose a dark dress of deep scarlet, along with my charcoal traveling cloak. Paired with black boots and a black cloche hat, it would be difficult to make me out from amongst the shadows.

I gave myself a glance in the mirror, and deeming my attire acceptable, made my way back out into the hall.

Miles looked up from his place leaning on the wall across from my door.

I smiled at him. "I half expected you to be gone already," I whispered in the dark silence of the hall.

He returned the smile, barely visible in the low light.

We went down the stairs, careful to avoid the second to last stair which housed a squeak that sounded rather charming by the light of day but might well wake a sleeping giant in the late hour.

"We will have to hope the butler will let us back in when we return," I murmured as I started toward the front door.

Miles did not follow me.

"What are you doing?" I asked.

"We should leave through the kitchens," he said. "The larder will likely have a door that we would be able to come back through."

"Do you really think the household staff will help us?" I asked. "Allowing us to sneak out after everyone else is asleep?"

"I have already spoken with the head cook," Miles said. "After dinner. I asked if she would be willing to spare me a key so that she would not have to wait up for me."

"And she agreed?" I asked. "She hardly knows you."

Miles shrugged. "I suppose a butler seems more trustworthy than others. We are held to a higher standard."

"I suppose that makes sense..." I said.

We made our way down toward the kitchens, passing

by some of the other servants' quarters and Elizabeth's father's study tucked away at the back of the house. I followed Miles down a narrow set of wooden stairs to the ground floor. The halls smelled of bread rising and cinnamon; breakfast had been being prepared for us for the next morning. My mouth watered; it had not been terribly long since I had eaten, but the excitement of going out and investigating again under the cover of darkness had quite obviously given me an appetite. *Perhaps once we arrive home, I can see if the cook would be willing to part with any of the leftover tarts that we enjoyed after dinner.*

The kitchen was empty apart from one woman wiping down the main prep area for the food, a long wooden table that spanned the back half of the room. Copper pots hung from the ceiling, and warmth emanated from the stove. "Good evening, Mrs. Cooper," Miles said, rapping against the wooden beam in the wall. "Might I still use your exit?"

Mrs. Cooper looked up from her scrubbing; it seemed that some flour had been upended on the table, caught in the cracks of the wooden board. She had kind eyes, with bushy hair that she had been tied up behind her neck with a green ribbon. "I suppose you can...though you did not mention that you would be bringing your mistress with you."

Miles smiled his easy grin. "I realize the late hour, but you must remember it is merely six in the evening for us. My lady is unable to sleep, and as such, I suggested a walk in the cool, night air."

Mrs. Cooper took a long look at me. "Neither of you seem particularly tired. If you would rather, I would be happy to make you up some glasses of warm milk or tea, so that you might not catch your death out in that cold."

"Thank you, truly, but I know my lady. We will not be gone long, perhaps just an hour. Once we have returned, she has assured me that she will be ready to sleep...except perhaps she may want to have something to sate her appetite."

"Certainly," Mrs. Cooper said. "I would be happy to find something. You said an hour, yes? That should give me enough time to finish preparing for the morning."

"That should be more than enough time," he said.

"Then allow me to see you out," Mrs. Cooper said, reaching into the front pocket of her apron and withdrawing a ring of keys. She started toward the door along the back wall.

She opened the door outside, letting the cold air in. I braced against it, as she stepped aside and let us pass. "Do take care," she said. "These streets are not as safe as they once were."

Miles nodded. "Duly noted, my good lady. And we shall let ourselves back in, if we return later than expected. I still have the key you loaned me earlier."

She gave him a wry smile, and closed the door behind us.

"Miles, what do you really think when people speak to you as if you are a butler?" I asked as we started through the narrow alley between Elizabeth's family home and the row house beside it.

He glanced at me. "Why should they not? I am a butler," he replied simply.

"Yes, but you are merely pretending for the time being," I said. "It must be difficult, being treated as a servant when you know deep down that you are innocent and have only resorted to acting this part out of sheer necessity."

We came to the mouth of the alley and stepped out onto the surprisingly bright street. Lead pained lampposts glowed a warm shade of gold, illuminating the sidewalks and the middle of the street as if dawn had already arrived.

Miles slowed his steps as we continued along the sidewalk toward the intersection up ahead. "I have never held any resentment, if that's what you're asking," he said, his voice low. "I accepted that this would be an inevitable part of my search, and to be perfectly honest, serving your family was far preferable to living on the streets as I had been. It was one of the few ways I was able to watch my cousin's movements without being spotted." He smiled, but it held no mirth. "A city such as New York, much like London, allows those of a more criminal nature to prowl the streets, almost entirely unnoticed."

I didn't know what to say. He had endured such hardships, the sort that no one should have to.

"If you are wondering if I have been mistreated by you or your family, you may put your mind at ease," Miles said. "Your father has been a fair employer. Your mother and sister have always been pleased with my character and sense of humor – "

"Not to mention your ability to anticipate the needs of everyone," I said with a bit of a laugh.

Half of a smile stretched up his face. "And you... well, you, Miss Sylvia...I have greatly enjoyed the time getting to know you. Since meeting you and working alongside you, it has been the first time since I lost my Sophia that I have felt as if I have purpose. That I have felt...happy."

I was grateful for the dark, as I knew my expression must betray my surprise at hearing him speak so plainly. "I...I am glad to hear it," I said.

We reached the intersection, and Miles glanced up and down the street. "I imagined we might run into some difficulty trying to find a cab at this hour so far removed from the city center."

"What should we do?" I asked. "I cannot imagine it would be all together wise to walk all the way there."

"It would take us hours," Miles said. "If we go south a few more blocks, then we should be able to find a more populated area, where some theaters and taverns are likely to still be entertaining people."

"Right," I said.

We crossed the street and continued on together. My eyes strained against the dark corners and shadows that the light from the lamps could not quite reach. Mrs. Cooper's words filled my mind, warning us of the danger. I reminded myself that I had been the one insistent on coming, and even if I found myself frightened, I did not like the idea of Miles being out here all alone, either.

We did manage to find a commercial street two blocks away, where we began to spot a few more people. We passed a couple perhaps a decade older than we, speaking in low voices, arm in arm. We found half a dozen young men whooping and calling leaving a pub on the corner, followed soon by three elderly gentlemen, one of whom barked out a laugh that made me jump.

Miles moved closer to me. "Do not worry. It is far too nice a neighborhood for there to be any riffraff here," he said. "These are ordinary people."

I nodded. "I suppose this city is still rather foreign to me," I said. "I am familiar with New York, and know what I should expect there. Here, though..."

"It all seems so strange," Miles said, his voice trailing off.

I realized it must be worse for him than it could

ever be for me. That his return to his home city must be dangerous and secret was surely difficult.

Miles managed to find a group of people standing together outside of the theaters, all of whom seemed to be waiting to call a cab. He reached up and flipped up the collar of his cloak, obscuring more of his face than the shadow from his hat already did.

"I noticed your unease when Elizabeth mentioned the party for her engagement tomorrow night," I said.

He nodded. He did not need to explain that it was out of fear that he might be recognized.

"What do you plan to do?" I asked, trying my best to keep my questions vague and unassuming for any nosy eavesdroppers around us.

"I do not think I should attend," he said. "I realize your friend may not take kindly to my decision, but you know as well as I that it might well be troublesome for me to be present."

"Right," I said. "If you would like, I would be happy to greet everyone on your behalf, and subtly see if perhaps any of them might be able to help us."

Miles gave me a sidelong look. "I suppose it is possible that one of them may have the...recipe that we are looking for, but you may also find it difficult to convince anyone to share their secrets with you."

"I see..." I said. "Yes, I suppose you're right. If they want to protect the original recipe writer, out of some sort of loyalty to him, then I shall need to proceed with caution."

"Most people will assume his recipe is the true one," Miles said. "Which makes my situation all the more difficult."

An older woman standing in front of us turned around to give Miles and me a questioning look through her thin spectacles. *Good thinking, Miles,* I thought. *Coming up with a reasonable word that we can both understand, but others around us will not.*

"I will take care not to step on any toes," I said. "If you are unable to attend, then I can do business in your stead."

Miles nodded as a pair of cabs pulled up along the sidewalk. The family in front of us walked to the taxi nearest to us, and Miles and I walked to the second.

Miles cleared his throat as the cabbie leaned out the window. "Where you headin'?"

"Good evening," Miles said.

I raised my eyebrows, and could not help the look I gave him. *Is that an American accent?* Or at least what might pass as one in any place that was not New York?

"We are hoping to make it to our friend's home in the Hyde Park area," he said, still maintaining a rather good hold on the accent. "Could you take us there, please?"

"Visiting from out of country, I see?" the cabbie asked.

"Yes, we are from New York," I said, leaning into Miles and laying my free hand on his arm. "Celebrating our engagement."

Miles grinned at me.

"Well, come on, then," the cabbie said, waving us in. "No sense in keeping me waiting here idle."

Miles opened the door and helped me in. I gave an exaggerated giggle as he sat down beside me, drawing a glance from the cabbie in the rearview mirror.

"How long you pair in town for?" the cabbie asked as he pulled away from the sidewalk.

"Two weeks," I said, smiling at Miles.

"And the wedding?" the cabbie asked.

"Yes?" Miles asked.

The cabbie chuckled. "Your wedding. When is it?"

"Oh, June," I said with another giggle. "We cannot wait."

"I cannot imagine that would escape anyone..." the cabbie said as we started off down the street toward Hyde Park.

Despite all of our cheerful tones, as I glanced out the darkened windows, at the city slipping by on either side of us, I suppressed a shiver. There was no telling what this night held in store or what dangers waited beyond the shadows.

4

———

"I have only been to Hyde Park once before," I said, almost offhanded, as the cabbie slowed to a stop at an intersection on the northern side of the river Thames. "When I was very young."

"Really?" Miles asked. It amazed me that he managed to maintain his artificial accent as long as he had. "Why don't you tell me about it?"

"I came to visit my grandparents on my mother's side, who lived here at the time. It was early spring, perhaps a month from now. My sister and I were so little that all I can remember is a kind man in a striped suit who gave the pair of us peppermint candies. It was a rare day where the sun stayed out all day, and we were able to lie in the grass and chew our candies with not a care in the world..."

Miles smiled at me, his green eyes searching my face.

My cheeks colored, and I wondered what in the world had come over me that I felt the need to share such an inconsequential story.

"I, too, have a love for this place..." Miles said, glancing out the window. Despite the dark, orbs of light from the lamps dotted around the park made the stretch of park seem as if it were filled with hovering stars. "It has been some time since I have seen it, but when I have been here in the past, my favorite pastime was to walk the grounds in the evenings."

"A wonderful time, to be certain," said our cabbie. "Be sure to have a stop there, during your trip. That way the two of you can make some more memories to take back home with you before the wedding."

"Of course, what a wonderful idea..." I said, giving Miles a smile. I knew it was out of the question, as the memories for Miles would do nothing good, and after so much time had passed, there would be nothing of value to investigate there anyway.

The cabbie pulled up just outside the park, as Miles had asked.

"Take care, you two," he said, leaning out the window, tipping the end of his cap to us. "I wish you the very best in your life together."

"Thank you very much, sir," Miles said. "We appreciate it."

"Of course," he said.

Miles paid him, and paid him well. He went on his way, and Miles watched him leave.

"Are you ready?" I asked.

"I suppose I have no choice now," Miles said, returning to his usual accent. "He's already left. Shall we?"

He turned and pointed down the street.

"My family's home is down this way," he said.

I fell into step beside him, wandering toward a part of the city that seemed far more luxurious than even Sutton Place where my family lived.

The rowhouses were of a beautiful, clean ivory. The windows, lead-paned, stretched taller than my own height, and lanterns hung beside each and every door along the street. The rooftops boasted gargoyles or cherubs; one house three down from the end of the street had an impressive statue of an angel between a pair of chimneys.

Miles barely looked up, keeping his gaze fixed on his house at the end of the street. Yet, as much as he must have felt like an outsider at this time, it suited him. How could I never have noticed it before?

I had always wondered about his poise, his polished manner, and how he had learned to carry himself so well among the wealthy. It came naturally to him, and I thought his experience must have far outweighed many in his profession. Knowing now that he was merely pretending to be a butler, that he was filling in a role to protect himself made a great deal of sense.

Watching him walk past these houses, wearing what he likely would have worn before he had been forced to flee London...he seemed to belong here.

My face flushed as I turned away. The longer we were here, the more Miles had begun to feel like a stranger to me.

It wasn't as if I could claim we were terribly close in the first place. He was our family butler, and as such, our relationship had only ever developed as far as that naturally would suggest. We might have had more unique circumstances, given the fact that he had helped me on multiple murder investigations, but so much had been pretend. His position, his reactions, all of them had to be filtered through the sieve of his circumstances, and that left me questioning how genuine the Miles I knew truly was in comparison to who he might have been before he fled.

"We are coming up on the street," Miles said. "There is a small park on the corner, just up ahead. We should be able to see the house from there. At the very least, we shall be able to see if there are any lights on inside."

"All right," I said. As quiet as the streets were, we might have been all alone in the city that night.

The park he indicated reminded me a great deal of

the little park near Sutton Place where we had once met my cousin Michael while he was on the run from the police. It was no larger than one of the rowhouses that it sat beside, dotted with a few small trees. Rose bushes had been trimmed neatly in a corner of the low walls that surrounded the park. We strode inside, and Miles offered me his arm. I obliged, knowing it would help our façade if anyone were to walk by, even at this late hour.

"It's the third house in the row," Miles said as he drew up to one of the low walls. He hovered near a thin, young tree, using the shadows cast by a streetlamp as extra cover.

I came up beside him, peering down the empty street.

It was a handsome home, to be certain, with large windows and a pair of flower boxes hanging beneath the front windows on the main floor. "It appears vacant," I said in a low voice. "I see no drapes in the windows, nor any sign of life on the front steps."

"Nor do I..." Miles said. "Which is odd, given what Mr. Walton said."

"Indeed," I agreed.

He reached into the front of his cloak, and withdrew a slim set of binoculars. He pressed them to his eyes. His forehead wrinkled as he studied the house that he had lived in so recently. I wanted to ask what he was thinking when he looked upon it, what he felt. I could imagine it was a myriad of emotions, from anger to sorrow to regret, perhaps even some joy. It must be hard to be so close to the home that was rightfully his, and be unable to approach it, to step inside.

"Are you all right?" I asked finally, unable to stop myself.

He lowered the binoculars. "I have dreamt of coming back here, looking over my house," he said. "I thought it would grieve me to see it again...but in truth, it just makes me feel rather relieved."

"Relieved?" I asked.

He nodded. "I have known all along that I was innocent, but to see my own home gives me hope that this is not all together lost."

"But...do you not think of your wife?" I asked, tentative.

He glanced at me, and to my surprise, a sad sort of smile spread across his face. "I miss Sophia...every day. But I came to realize months ago that nothing I did could change the past. Sophia did not deserve what happened, but all I can do now is to set it right and clear my own name and ensure that her killer is brought to justice."

"It must have taken a great deal of struggle to reach that conclusion," I murmured.

He sighed, exhaling through his nose. "I have spent a great many nights awake, considering this. Being angry will not bring her back. Nothing I do will. She is gone, and I can do her honor by cherishing her memory, but not allowing myself to remain in a pit of grief. She would have wished for me to continue on with my life, and to try and move on."

"A generous woman," I said. "I suppose in life, some might not be as kind as to wish their husbands the same happiness."

He smirked. "Oh, she would not have taken kindly to me imagining life with anyone else, or anything of that sort..." he said. "But if the situation had been different, and she was the one who was still standing here and not me, I would have wished her the utmost happiness...and I would not have wanted her to go through life alone."

My face burned as he looked over at me.

"She would forgive me if I fell in love again..." he said.

For a moment, we stood there staring at one another, and all I could hear was the thumping of my own heart in my ears.

"Look – " Miles said, lifting the binoculars once more and pointing back toward the house. "The window on the second floor, the second from the right. That used to be my study, and I had a lamp with a green glass shade sitting right in that window. It's gone, now."

I squinted through the dark, but I could not make

out any distinct shape in the window. "Do you suppose that your cousin has moved it?"

"I wonder, indeed," he said. "If he has begun moving in his own belongings..."

"What should we do?" I asked. "Would it be wise to get any closer?"

"I fear that he may have left people inside to keep an eye on the place," Miles said. "If he has, then we could be spotted if we linger too long nearby."

"Do you suppose they will see us here?" I asked.

"I doubt it," Miles said. "We are far enough away, and this park sees many visitors on a daily basis."

"All right," I said. "Then what?"

"We should make our way behind the house."

"Less of a chance of being spotted by someone through a main window, possibly?" I asked.

"Yes," he said. I noticed the hard set of his jaw, and the wrinkling of his forehead. I always thought Miles looked rather young; in that moment, in the late hour, he seemed to have aged many years in just a matter of moments.

We made our way across the street and then down a narrow passage between the rowhouses, to the same sort of alleyway as the one behind Elizabeth's family home. I hardly saw these small pathways used for deliveries, for the servants to come and go without using the front entrance. In London, the pathways ran tight; if I spread my arms wide, I might be able to touch both buildings along either side.

"I cannot believe that my parents would have allowed this to happen..." Miles said, rolling his shoulders as we wandered down the alley, his boots crunching the gravel beneath his feet. "To let Felton come in and take the house away from me..."

Felton...at least I know his name now, I thought.

Miles huffed, adjusting his hat as if it squeezed his head too tightly. "I suppose this must mean they really believe me gone...or perhaps dead," he said. "Which means they must believe that I really did kill her."

I did not have the heart to argue with him about whether or not his parents would truly have believed such a thing. I couldn't speak for someone I did not know. At the moment, I felt as if I hardly knew Miles.

Regardless, it must have been agonizing to think such things of his own family.

I suppose I know about that in my way, I thought. *Everyone in my family wanted to do everything they could to ignore what their eyes were telling them about my uncle's murder. It seems that no one truly knows anyone until they are put into such difficult circumstances.*

"We must keep quiet," Miles whispered, his voice almost lost in the gentle breeze brushing through the alleyway. "There are fewer chances of being spotted this way, but there is a window into the kitchens. I should like to see what has changed within, if anything."

He pocketed his binoculars once again, and started toward the outer wall, his back against the wall. As he went off toward the house, I followed suit.

My heart beat rapidly against my chest, and my palms began to sweat. I knew full well that this house belonged to Miles, and therefore, what we were doing could not truly be considered trespassing. However, if we were caught, then there was little chance of us escaping without him being arrested. If he were arrested, then I would be on my own to investigate the murder.

Miles looked to me, and lifted a finger to his lips. He bent into a crouch, and eased himself against the wall beside a window on the ground floor.

I had yet to see a light streaming through any of these windows, but that didn't mean there was not anyone inside. Miles had said that he would have expected his cousin to have left someone there to watch the place. I should have asked him; what was his plan? Did he mean to go inside the house? Or merely to see it with his own eyes?

He leaned around the edge of the window shutter, and his lingering gave me comfort that he had yet to see anyone.

"I hardly spent a moment in this part of the house..." Miles murmured, ducking and moving to the other side of the window so that I might look in as well. "Which now strikes me as a terrible miss. I have spent more time in the kitchens of your family's home than I believe I ever did in my own home as a child."

"You never wandered down to the kitchens as a child looking for sweets?" I whispered.

He spared me a brief look, before he returned to peering through the darkened window. "No, I never did. Even out on our country estate, I preferred to be in the stables with my father. I wanted to spend as much time with the horses as I could."

"Oh, I absolutely loved visiting the kitchens," I said. "Gibbins has been our house chef since I was five, and he always saved a small portion of the desserts he made to give me. Anything with honey in it, especially."

Miles smiled at me. "Gibbins is quite a character. I have greatly enjoyed getting to know him."

"I am glad to hear that," I said.

His smile faded. "I never realized how much I took the house staff for granted," he said. "It is part of the reason why I wanted to do my job as your family's butler to the best of my ability. I am thankful that I had the chance."

"It seems that it was fate that we met that night," I said.

"I have not doubted it for a moment," he said.

I turned to gaze into the darkened kitchen. It

certainly appeared more antiquated than our kitchen at home, but that may have been due to the age of the house. Mother had insisted that we upgrade the stove and the prep station in our own home so that Gibbins could hire some more help, which certainly improved the quality of life for many. By contrast, Miles' kitchen seemed smaller, but had a classic charm with the ceramic pitchers neatly arranged on a nearby shelf, a wash basin with a pump beneath the window, and an enormous old stove along one wall.

"Does it look different?" I whispered.

"No..." Miles said, his brow furrowing again. "Which is what troubles me. He would have surely wanted *his* things in the house, and not a thing of mine to remain. Why wouldn't he have begun to change the items that he would use on a daily basis, items he would use to eat with?"

"I don't – "

A flash of light appeared in the corner of the kitchen, bouncing off the side wall. It took me a moment to realize that it was through a doorway at the back of the room, likely leading to the rest of the house.

I gasped, and pulled away from the window, but it was not before the light swung into the kitchen and shone directly at the glass behind which Miles and I were standing.

Miles crouched again, practically rolling beneath

the window as he reached out and grabbed my hand. "Run!" he exclaimed.

I clung to his hand and pushed myself on as quickly as I could. Light glanced off the opposite wall on the back of the other rowhouses in an erratic fashion.

My breath came in harsh pants as we neared the end of the alleyway.

A shout reached us, and Miles ran even harder. "Hey! Stop, you thieves!"

We did not stop running until we reached the other side of the park. Miles collapsed into one of the benches, and I knelt over beside him, hands on my knees.

"That...was close," he breathed, lifting his hat from his head, running his fingers through his blonde hair.

"Do you...know who...that was?" I asked between gasps.

He shook his head, then patted the bench beside him. "Come and sit. You should – you should catch your breath."

I nodded, taking a seat beside him. My thighs burned from the effort. "I haven't...run that fast...since I was a child."

He laughed, but it sounded pained.

"So you don't know...who that was?" I asked again.

"No," Miles said. "He must be someone my cousin hired."

"I suppose that is further proof that he has something to hide," I said.

"Perhaps," he said. He swiped the back of his hand across his face. "All right. We need to go back. We have seen all that we can tonight."

"I'm sorry we didn't find anything you were looking for," I said.

"You may be surprised to hear that I think we did find something..." he said, getting up from the bench. "I now know that my cousin has been in the house, already changing some things, hiring guards or staff or whoever they are. It indicates he is trying to protect the house."

"And therefore, trying to cover up his heinous acts," I said.

He nodded. "That is my suspicion as well."

He held his hand out to me, and I took it.

"We can call a cab from the park once again," he said.

"All right," I said.

I glanced down at our hands, and my face flushed pink. This had somehow become a common occurrence, something that I no longer hesitated about. Since my learning the truth about him, he had become even more comfortable with the action, with pretending to be affectionate with one another, making any passersby believe we were together. Walking arm in arm with him had almost become like second nature.

What does this mean? I wondered. Perhaps it meant nothing...

I looked up at him as we started off, and immediately I could see he had become lost in thought. I did not wish to disturb him, as he deserved the chance to think through this difficult situation. Nevertheless, it seemed to be growing easier and easier to watch him, knowing that I no longer had to suspect him of murder.

Careful, now, Sylvia...he is still very much in love with his wife. She is the whole reason he is trying so desperately to solve this case.

I knew that. I knew it full well. It did not mean that I couldn't still be pleased that he was innocent, that I couldn't continue to be fond of him as I had always found myself to be.

Fond of him...is that really all?

I supposed it did not matter if it was more. There was nothing that could be done.

5

———

"Elizabeth, would you prefer this garland here?" I asked from the third step of a ladder. I held a long strand of ivy that had been sewn together, mingled with dried roses and spearmint to make the room fragrant.

Elizabeth, standing near the door to the dining room and speaking with her butler, turned to look up at me. "Oh, that is a wonderful place. Thank you, Sylvia."

I nodded, and finished tying the end of the garland to the top of a bureau. I took care in walking down the ladder, and stepped back to look at my work. It had been too short to hang over the mantle, and Elizabeth had considered bringing it to the foyer to find a place for it. I, instead, noticed a rather similar gap between the pair of bureaus along the back wall of the dining room, and took charge of the decoration to see if it would fit. And it did so, quite nicely, in fact.

We had gotten to work first thing that morning getting the house sorted for the party. We had started in the drawing room where I had helped her arrange some games to play, as well as a table for gifts should her family decide to bring any. Then we moved to the sunroom, where smaller tables had been set up for tea that evening after dinner. She had chosen to hang slender crystals from the windows, which sparkled in the light of the grey morning, and also stole some of the warm, golden glow from the flickering fire.

By the time lunch rolled around, Elizabeth had accomplished a great deal of her tasks, along with the help of the butler and a few of the maids. Tea sets were chosen and laid out in the sunroom; dining sets polished and placed on the table; chairs moved and tables shifted around for the comfort of the guests.

"That really was rather clever of you," Elizabeth said, gesturing to the garland. "It brings warmth to this side of the room."

"I suppose it is worthwhile to have another pair of eyes looking at the same problem," I said.

"Or perhaps someone who is not quite as nervous as I am..." she said.

I smiled. "What do you have to be nervous about?" I asked. "Mr. Walton is wonderful. Your family is sure to love him."

"It isn't Peter that I am worried about..." she said, laying a hand on her heart. "I suppose a party like this just makes it all the more real, does it not?"

"It does, I would say," I said. "But I thought this was what you wanted."

She shook her head. "Oh, I am muddling this all up. Of course it is what I want. I want nothing more than to marry Peter...but how do I know that I will be any good as a wife?"

I gave her a warm smile that I hoped came across as understanding. "My dear friend, you have nothing to worry about."

"How can you be so certain?" she asked.

"Because I know you," I said with a chuckle. "You are caring, thoughtful, and have a good sense of humor. What more could any man want? Anyone can see how Mr. Walton already adores you."

She looked at me even as some of the servants behind her set crystal glasses down upon the table, or laid napkins folded like swans onto the bone china plates. "Oh? What makes you such an expert in matters of love?" she asked.

The blood rose to my cheeks. "I – Come now, Elizabeth. I do not know what you are talking about."

She smirked at me. "You most certainly do know. Clearly, you have fallen in love yourself and do not wish to admit it."

I looked away, reaching for another garland...but

found the corner of the table where we had been keeping them empty. "What nonsense," I said.

"Is it?" she asked. "I have seen the way you look at your friend Miles."

"Elizabeth, he is my family's butler," I said, giving her a pointed look. *That may be true, but as soon as you find the right evidence, everything will change and you will no longer be able to use that excuse,* a small voice at the back of my mind reminded me.

"You say that, and yet, he does not seem to *act* much like a servant, does he?" she asked.

"I disagree. He is quite good at his job," I said, trying to find something to do with my hands while she looked at me with those knowing eyes of hers. "Mother always says that he has somehow learned to anticipate her needs before she even speaks them."

"Even if that is so..." Elizabeth said. "Has it not crossed your mind that he is simply trying to impress your family in order to please you?"

"What a preposterous suggestion," I said.

"I don't think it is. I have seen the way he looks at you when you do not know he is looking," she said.

"You don't understand," I said. "He is in love with someone else. Has been for years now."

She glanced at me. "Has he told you that?"

"He...he has told me that there was someone very dear to him," I said. "Before he lost her."

"Well, then, I should think it would be obvious that

he has forgotten her and fallen in love with you." She turned and started toward the table where some more of the dried flowers she had used for the garland lay spread out across the surface. With a keen eye, she began to select a number of them with long stems.

"He has not forgotten her," I said. "He has spoken of her so recently..."

"He might just be trying to be vulnerable with you," she said, moving a beautiful yellow rose to the back of those she held in her hands. "He wants you to know him better."

Could that be true? He had told me so little of his past that I hardly knew him, but she was right...he seemed to be trying to help me understand him better lately.

"I believe part of the reason he has come to England is in order to figure out what he wishes to do in regards to the woman he loved and lost," I said.

"Yes, I imagine he plans to put it all behind him," Elizabeth said. "Where is he, by the by?" She tilted her head to both sides as she surveyed her flower arrangement. "I have not yet seen him this morning, unless my fiancé has busied him with something."

"Oh..." I said. "To be honest, I do not believe he was feeling terribly well this morning."

Elizabeth frowned, looking at me. "What a shame. It must be all that traveling."

I nodded, thankful that she had supplied the idea

herself instead of forcing me to lie. "I think that is certainly part of it, yes."

She shook her head. "I have never done well with traveling across the ocean," she said. "It always left me feeling unwell for days afterward. Even weeks, depending on the severity of the waves when on board."

"I have never known him to be so weak of constitution, but he did not look as if he had gotten a great deal of sleep last night," I said, which was the honest truth. The circles beneath his eyes told me that he must have stayed up far later than even I had upon returning to Elizabeth's home.

"Nor do you, but I did not wish to say anything," Elizabeth said with yet another smirk.

"I'm sorry to say that I do not believe he will be in attendance this evening for the party," I said. "When I checked on him after lunch, he had laid himself up in bed."

"Shall I send my butler up to him?" Elizabeth asked.

"No, I think all he really wants is rest," I said. "Perhaps it would be best not to disturb him for the time being."

"All right, then," Elizabeth said. "Still...if he needs anything, you need only ask."

"Thank you," I said. "I do appreciate it."

We spent the rest of the hour finishing another pair

of flower arrangements to use up the rest of the dried flowers, and then Elizabeth departed to ready herself for the evening. She asked if I would be willing to go and help her with her hair, which I agreed to. I had helped to arrange Joan's hair before her plays more than enough times to have at least some idea what I was doing.

As the time for the party drew nearer, my nerves hummed all the more. Miles had chosen to sit out the party so as not to risk being recognized by anyone in attendance. This would be my chance to mingle and listen, in the hopes that I could catch some information that he would be unable to.

"You look stunning this evening," I told Elizabeth as I helped to clasp a strand of pearls around her neck, the final piece of her outfit. "Mr. Walton is going to ask you to marry him all over again."

Elizabeth turned, blushing herself. "You really think so?"

"Indeed," I said. I had managed a halfway decent plait, which I tied up behind her head. I pinned it in place with some crystals pins, and so far, it seemed to be holding.

"Oh, Sylvia..." she said, beaming at me. "When Father and Mother moved us here, I had every intention of coming back to New York when I was old enough. I never thought that I could marry one of these stodgy, stuffy British men. Peter surprised me, though. He is precisely what I needed, and easily won me over."

"I am happy that you found someone who fits you so well," I said. "Shall we go down and greet your guests?" I gestured toward the door.

"One moment..." Elizabeth said. She got up and walked to her wardrobe. She opened it and reached within, withdrawing a lovely jewelry box with a cross-stitched top. She brought it back, setting it down upon the table where she had set out her accessories for the evening.

She lifted the top and pulled out a beautiful golden chain, which held a simple ruby charm. Something about it seemed familiar. She smiled at it before passing it toward me.

"What's this?" I asked.

"For you to wear," she said, still smiling. "This is one of my favorite pieces. It's rather simple, I know, but I thought it would match your dress this evening. I know Miles will not be joining us, but if you have the chance to see him later...well, I thought he might find it almost as pretty as you."

She walked around me without waiting for an answer, and I lifted my hair so that she might fasten it behind my neck. She laughed gently.

"What is so funny?" I asked, laying my hand against the charm.

"You do not recognize it?" she asked. "You gave me this necklace for my twelfth birthday."

My eyes widened, and I whirled around to her. "I thought I recognized it!"

She beamed at me. "It is still one of my favorite pieces. I wear it all the time. Come along now, my mother will wonder what is taking us so long up here."

We started down the stairs, and the hum of the voices of the guests rose up to greet us like the smoke of a comforting fire.

I thought it best to take a chance now while the question would seem inconspicuous. "Who has come this evening?" I asked. "Are there any guests that I might know?"

"Oh, you may well know some, such as my aunt and uncle from Pennsylvania who moved here when my parents and I did," Elizabeth said. "Though most of the family has lived here all along. Cousins and some friends. It should not be more than two dozen people this evening. Our wedding shall be a large enough event, and I do not think Mother could handle two large events so close together."

"I see," I said. "I really do wish we could have planned our trip better, that we might have been here to celebrate your wedding with you."

She reached out and pulled me closer to her. "Sylvia, you need not worry. You have come early during a time when I can truly spend time with you. If you were here closer to the wedding, then I might not have had a chance to spend any time with you at all." She grinned. "Truly, this is preferable to me. Who knows what sort of witch I will be closer to the wedding day."

I smirked, but said, "It's not possible. You are going to be a serene bride, with no trouble at all, not an ounce of stress – "

The pair of us began to laugh as we reached the bottom of the stairs.

Mr. Walton stood at the bottom, and turned to peer up at us. "Well, it certainly seems as if the pair of you are having a good time this evening," he said.

Elizabeth parted from me to join her fiancé near the door so they could greet guests who still filtered into the house. "As we always do," she said.

"I must admit, Miss Sylvia, I wish that my Elizabeth had a friend as dear as yourself who lived here in London," Mr. Walton said as Elizabeth joined arms with him. "Might I be able to convince you to stay?"

I smiled. "You are far too kind. As much as I love Elizabeth and this city, I fear that I would never quite fit in. Not only that, but my sister would never forgive me for leaving her behind."

"Then she could join us," Mr. Walton said with a chuckle. "I would do anything to help Elizabeth be as happy all the time as she has been during your stay here with us thus far."

"Darling, I suppose this means that we shall have to make a trip to New York in the near future," Elizabeth said, tapping her chin. "Perhaps we could extend our honeymoon?"

He beamed at her. "For you, my dear? We could do it."

"That settles it, then," Elizabeth said to me. "We shall have to go and see you to continue our jolly visit."

"I am certain my parents would be pleased to have you," I said. "And it would give you the chance to see some of our other school friends, and show Mr. Walton around some of the places where you grew up."

"Precisely," Elizabeth said with a grin. "This is perfect."

"We shall make plans during your stay," Mr. Walton said to me. "I imagine your family would prefer more than a few weeks' notice – "

A couple entered through the door, and Elizabeth let out a delighted "Hello!"

I smiled at Mr. Walton. "I shall leave you both to greet your guests."

"Please do go and help yourself to some refreshments in the drawing room," Mr. Walton murmured as Elizabeth embraced the middle-aged woman who had come in, who had a nose quite similar to hers. "We shall join you soon."

I departed the foyer and wandered down the hall toward the growing sounds of conversation in the drawing room. A number of Elizabeth's family members were already in attendance, gathering around the buffet table along the wall or at the windows overlooking the city streets. A man with a round belly near the fireplace laughed aloud, his whole body jiggling. The rail of a woman that stood with him chortled behind her gloved, boney hand. *I suppose there would be a great deal of people in her family that I have never met, those who have lived here in London,* I thought.

A woman around my mother's age stood near the door, swirling a tiny silver spoon in her teacup. She smiled at me as I passed by.

Half a dozen family members stood around Elizabeth's father, who seemed already deep into a story from his time in the military, one of his favorite pastimes. I smiled as I wandered over to the end of the buffet where Elizabeth and I had decided to have the punchbowl set up. It was a recipe that Gibbins used every year for our family birthdays, and Elizabeth's cook seemed all too eager to have something made for her instead of having to come up with one on her own. I dipped the ladle in and scooped some of the icy beverage into a crystal cup set aside for it. I made sure to scoop up some of the apple slices that we had asked the cook to scatter on top.

I turned to survey the room, and pursed my lips as I raised the sweet, subtly tangy smelling punch to my nose. It seemed that Miles' decision to wait until nightfall to sneak out to look for information might have proven to be more useful than my own mission. Looking around, it did not appear as if these were the sorts of people that would have any information pertaining to his wife's murder.

*Perhaps this is not as helpful as I hoped it would be...*I thought.

"Pardon me, Miss," said a voice nearby. "Are you one of Mr. Walton's relations?"

I looked up to see a young couple, likely around my age, standing at the buffet. The young man, dark-haired and bright eyed, smiled as he scooped up some punch into a glass for him and the woman with him, who had hair like spun copper.

"Oh, no, I am one of Elizabeth's friends, visiting from New York," I said with a smile.

The young woman's eyes widened, and immediately, I thought I recognized her. "How very interesting," she said. "I am Elizabeth's cousin Victoria, and this is my husband Ralph."

"How do you do?" he asked, holding his cup aloft in greeting.

"I thought I recognized you," I said with a smile. "You are not from London, are you?"

She grinned. "Not originally, no," she said. "My parents moved me here when I was about ten."

"We met a few times when we were much, much younger," I said. "My name is Sylvia Shipman."

Victoria's eyes widened. "Well, I'll be..." she said. "I do remember you! We met at one of Elizabeth's birthday parties, where we rode the ponies!"

"Yes," I said with a laugh.

"How nice it is to see you again," Victoria said. She looked at her husband. "This is one of Lizzie's dearest friends. They have been close since they were in primary school."

"And you are here to celebrate her engagement?" Ralph asked.

"Yes," I said. "It was high time I made the trip here to visit her, anyway. It seemed the perfect time."

"How wonderful," Victoria said. "How long are you here for?"

"Just two weeks," I said. "Not a great deal of time, but I did not wish to overstay my welcome when there are still so many wedding plans to be getting on with."

"Oh, what a shame," Ralph said. "Not nearly enough time to see the city to its full extent."

"Such as the museums," Victoria said.

"Or the restaurants," Ralph added with a knowledgeable nod.

"And it is unfortunate that you will not be able to attend some of the spring festivities that are coming in the weeks ahead," Victoria said. "Are you one for social gatherings, Sylvia?"

*Social gatherings? I wonder if I might be able to direct the conversation...*I thought. "I am certainly well acquainted with them," I said. "What sort of festivities?"

"Well, let's see..." Ralph said. "There is the charity auction at the Cummings estate in April," he counted on his fingers.

"And do not forget the McMurray's ball set for just before Easter," Victoria said.

Ralph's eyes widened. "Oh, well there is the Beech-wood weekend gathering that happens every month, but that is near impossible to get an invitation to these days – "

My heart dropped right to the floor. "Did you say Beechwood?" I asked. I could hardly dare to believe it. What were the chances?

"Do you know the name?" Victoria asked.

"I am familiar with it, yes," I said. "At least, I have heard of it."

"That is of little surprise," Ralph said with a chor-tle. "It is quite the name in London. Prominent family, though it has become rather infamous in the last few years..."

"How so?" I asked.

"Oh, of course you wouldn't know," Victoria said. "Well, it is said that one of the Beechwoods, the orig-inal heir to the family's estates, killed his wife."

"You don't say," I said with as much surprise as I could muster.

She nodded enthusiastically. "Indeed. This monthly weekend retreat is not hosted by the supposed killer, but his cousin who supposedly was his closest friend."

"How heartbreaking it must have been for him," I said, careful to keep my true emotions from showing on my face.

"I can only imagine how tragic the whole affair must have been for the family," she said.

"The parties are some of the most exclusive in the city," said Ralph. "Which is why I should not have even suggested it, or allowed you to get your hopes up with false pretenses of having the chance of being invited."

"Oh..." I said. "Well, I suppose that's all right. Why would anyone want to invite a complete stranger in the first place?"

"Well, I certainly wouldn't say that," Victoria said. "It has nothing to do with you or your character, rather the sort of guests that make the guest list in the first place."

"Only the most prominent are invited personally, and occasionally they find someone they find interesting to attend," Ralph went on. "Members of parliament, bankers, aristocrats of all stripes..."

"I do not really know how much I believe the exclu-

sivity of it all," Victoria said. "How can we be certain it
is not nothing more than a fish tale?"

"It very well may be," Ralph said. "Effective,
though, I must say."

"Well, regardless, there is sure to be something that
you can do during your time here," Victoria said.
"Unless my cousin has you working the entire time."

"Oh, no, certainly not," I said with a smile. "She has
been very kind to me. I am still recovering after the
journey, if I am honest. My traveling companion is laid
up in bed after feeling seasick for almost a week."

"Oh, what a shame," Victoria said. "Well, perhaps if
I have the chance to speak with Elizabeth tonight, I can
convince her that we must have dinner while you are
in town. What do you say to that, dear?"

"I think that sounds wonderful," Ralph said with a
genuine smile that surprised me. He had only just met
me, and she and I had met only a few times as
children.

"Thank you," I said, my heart warming. "I appreciate it very much."

Elizabeth and Mr. Walton entered the room then,
to the applause of everyone in the room. The love they
received from their family made me quite happy to see.
Elizabeth deserved all the happiness she had found,
and I hoped the very best for the pair of them.

I withdrew toward the back of the room, giving her
a chance to greet the rest of her family that had

perhaps slipped in while she was speaking to others. She made her way around the room, introducing Mr. Walton to the doting people, all of whom hugged and cooed over him.

The clock struck seven not far behind me. I glanced at it. Miles might have snuck out again already, given the fact that night had already fallen.

*Be careful, Miles...*I thought. *There is no telling what dangers you could be walking into out there.*

6

I glanced out the door for what must have been the tenth time that minute. I could have sworn that I had caught a glimpse of something out of the corner of my eye, some movement that indicated that he had finally, *finally* returned to the house.

I breathed out through my nose, a long, anxious exhale as I tried to settle back into the rather small desk chair I had pulled around to face the door. A solitary lamp glowed on the desk, out of direct sight of the hall. As Miles and I had been placed in the guest halls, Elizabeth and her family would have to pass through the corridor in order to reach the upper floors where their quarters were. I did not want to give anyone cause for alarm if they passed by my room and saw that I was still awake, my door still wide open.

I turned my gaze to the book lying open on my lap, and pinched my burning eyes shut. I must have tried to read the same paragraph a dozen times, but had yet to retain even a word of what I had read.

The party had ended almost three hours ago, with Elizabeth saying goodnight to me almost two hours later. When I finally had the chance to peer into Miles' room, it astounded me that he had yet to return. I had not even been certain if he had left the house. I wandered down to ask the cook, who informed me that he had snuck out just after the party had started.

I snapped the book closed and laid it on the bedspread beside me, kicking my legs down from where I had propped them up on the bed. Did he not realize the worry that he had left me with? Did he truly think that I would not have been wondering where he was, especially as the clock inched toward midnight?

I sighed, puffing my cheeks out in exasperation. I drummed my fingers on the desk before I got to my feet to pace the floor.

I had a decision to make before he returned. The party I had learned about. Was it an event that his cousin had been hosting for a long time? Or did he start it after Miles' wife died? That would hardly make sense, which would mean that Miles would surely know about these parties.

If he wanted this to be an option, would he not have

mentioned it? I wondered. *I do not think he will take kindly to the idea that I would like to try and get an invitation...*

It would be the perfect means by which to look through his cousin's house. There truly would be no sense in missing this opportunity. How else could we possibly discover things that might be hidden in his place of residence? And it would be all the better because he would not know me, would have no reason to assume that I had any association with Miles.

And a whole weekend... I thought. *A weekend should be more than enough time for me to poke around, as long as I am able to get away unnoticed.*

I knew that it could present difficulties, though. Miles would not be able to get anywhere near his cousin without being recognized; he would know him the moment he laid eyes on him.

I stopped my pacing, and glanced out into the hall; I could have sworn that I had heard footsteps on the stairs again. After waiting a few moments, I resisted the urge to groan.

There were two issues with trying to find a way to get an invitation to this party. The first was that it would be cutting into my time with Elizabeth. It would mean leaving her for a few days when I only had two weeks with her in the first place.

I quickly absolved myself of the guilt as I reminded myself that I was here with Miles to help clear his name, not for a pleasure trip. That might have been the façade, and I might still very well hurt Elizabeth if I went off on my own for a few days, but it was, at the moment, more important for me to do. *I suppose it would be simple enough to tell her that we are going to visit some of Miles' family,* I thought. *That would not be entirely untrue. But where would Miles go? He could not very well come to the party.*

I would have to figure out what to do about that.

The second issue I saw was the invitation itself. According to Elizabeth's cousin, it was nigh impossible to receive one.

Frustrated, I resumed my path of pacing back and forth across the handsomely decorated guest room. How would I be able to find a connection in the time I would need to in order to garner an invite? And why would his cousin deem me important enough to receive one?

I chewed on my lip. Would this require having to create another character that would be worthy of such an invitation? Or would the people that I knew already here in London be able to point me in the direction of those who would be able to introduce me?

I didn't quite know which would be the best way forward, but I needed to talk to Miles.

"Miles, where are you?" I murmured.

I sat down and attempted to read once again,

picking up my book and forcing myself to try and focus on the page so I could pass the time as I waited.

I only had to wait for another fifteen minutes before I heard noise downstairs, my ears perking up. I lifted my head, shifting my itching eyes toward the doorway.

Miles swept by my room without even looking in, his eyes cast toward the floor.

I jumped up from the chair I had pulled to the bedside, tossing the book onto the bed as I hurried out of the room.

"Miles," I said, trying to keep my voice low.

He did not even turn around to look as he entered his own bedroom.

"Miles?" I said, a little louder.

He made to close his door behind him just as I slipped my hand into the door, stopping him.

His head snapped around, his bottle green eyes wide...before they registered who they were looking at. His shoulders sagged, and he let out a sharp sigh. "Sylvia..." he murmured. "What are you still doing awake?"

"Waiting for you," I said, pushing the door wider. "I could not possibly sleep until I knew you were all right."

"I'm fine," he said, dismissive, turning away.

"You're fine?" I asked, moving further into his room and closing the door behind me. "What did you find?"

He let out another heaving sigh, sinking down onto the bench at the end of his bed. He tugged off his boots, his expression sour. "It seems that what your friend spoke of and what we saw for ourselves last night ended up being the truth. My cousin has been making the effort to take possession of the house."

I eased myself into the desk chair in front of his desk. "Has he done so fully yet?"

"I do not believe so," he said. "I went down to some of the pubs that my servants used to frequent when I lived here, and found out there has been more activity in the house as of late, especially within the past few weeks."

"That does seem strange," I said, my brow furrowing. "Did anyone happen to know why?"

He grimaced as he pulled his gloves off his fingers, each finger one by one. "That is the troubling part," he said. "It seems that my cousin has become suspicious that someone is following him."

My eyes widened. "He knows you are after him?"

"I know that he knows I am still alive," Miles said. "And he must realize it would only be a matter of time before I figured out what really happened."

"But does anyone else know that it's you?" I asked.

He shook his head. "The gentleman I spoke with tonight happens to know one of the mail carriers who works on my old street. He told me it seems that Felton has been watching his back, becoming paranoid in his business dealings. He hardly ever makes a public appearance these days."

"That does seem strange..." I said. "Surely he would have had to tell someone, share his concerns with someone."

"I imagine he has, but it's a question of whether anyone will believe him," he said. "There are many people in London who think me dead. They might think he lost his mind, imagining he was seeing a ghost."

"I don't suppose that has done his reputation any good," I said.

"No, it very likely has not," Miles said, tossing his boot into the corner, scowling at it as if it had affronted him. "Our family name alone may well be all that is keeping him afloat at this point."

"So, if he is no longer making many public appearances and is backing out of business deals..." I said, looking at him. "This all centers around you, doesn't it?"

"And doing what he did," Miles said, stretching his arms high over his head. "I think the guilt is finally getting the better of him, and he has figured out I am following him. He likely realized it sometime in New York, and that is why he has come home to London to line everything up, put it behind him."

My brows knit together. "That makes little sense, though, does it? Even if he took possession of every bit of your inheritance, would he not lose it when he was proven guilty?"

"Yes..." Miles said, sounding reluctant. "Though it will be a great deal more difficult."

"Even if it is without doubt?" I asked. "Surely no one in their right mind would allow him to keep such wealth."

"People often do not wish to go after those of prominent stature," Miles said, looking up at me through his dark eyelashes. "It becomes rather sticky, not to mention how easy it is for those who suspect the truth to be bought off. The worst part is that he may well know I am in London again already. At this point, getting anywhere near him will be almost impossible."

I hesitated for a moment. I knew that I should mention the party, but now might not be the best time. "Well...it seems the only answer we have now is that I will have to be the one to do the – "

"No," Miles said flatly, getting to his feet. "That is out of the question."

I planted my hands on my hips. "Really, Miles, you cannot be so stubborn," I said. "We only have twelve more days here in London, and you cannot get close to your cousin yourself. No one in your family knows me, so I could – "

"Sylvia, I still do not think you understand," he said. "He killed Sophia without thought. Without fear.

What makes you think he would not do the same to you when he finds out that you are working with me?"

"You seem to forget that I have been in this situation before," I said. "I am not as helpless or unprepared as you seem to think."

He heaved a sigh. "I have not forgotten," he said. "And I do not think you incapable. All I want is to protect you from someone I know to be dangerous."

"They all have been dangerous," I said. "We simply did not know until after the fact."

He shook his head.

"You have a greater vested interest in this situation," I said. "Which I understand. As such, it has made you unable to think of anything else."

"But this is my responsibility," Miles said. "It should be me. Sophia was my wife, the murder was made to look as if I did it. I do not wish for you to be in harm's way."

"Yes, but would it not be better for you to have help?" I asked. "There is no reason why you have to take this on all alone."

He looked sad, more than anything.

"If I am the only one out of the two of us who can go out into the open, then why not use me?" I asked. "It would be far more productive. Remember when I discovered that an artist from whom I had commissioned a portrait had killed someone at the gallery?" I asked. "I went to his studio and got him to confess it to me. After some looking into it, I – "

"But you were reckless," he interrupted. "You never should have gone all alone to the studio that night. I should have gone with you, and you would not have been cornered like you were."

My face colored, but I pressed on. "What of the case I took on out in Rhode Island?" I asked. "I managed to find out, without any real help, that one of my new acquaintances out there had killed his own sister."

"If I recall, you told me later that you wished you had taken your cousin with you so you would not have been alone when you confronted the murderer," Miles said.

"I did," I said. "He was just downstairs while I spoke with the culprit. He went and collected the police for me."

"But you were in danger again," Miles said, shaking his head.

"Sometimes being in danger is unavoidable," I said. "I have not come all this way with you for nothing."

He sighed again, sinking back down onto the bench in front of his bed. "You have made your argument, and perhaps you are right. I have allowed myself to become too focused on the problem at hand, and forgotten how to best proceed. You have acted brilliantly in all of the cases that you have taken on. I simply do not wish to put you at risk on my account."

"I appreciate that," I said. "But the truth must come to light. You deserve to have the life you were meant to, with your family and your inheritance. There is no reason why you should have to live as a butler when the truth is that you have done nothing wrong. Your cousin will have to pay for his actions, and they will all see that you are innocent."

"I hope so..." he said.

I debated once again about asking him what his plans for the future were, but it seemed I had just laid them out for him. He would likely come back to New York with me to share the news with my family, but then would return to London to live.

*And it only makes sense...*I thought, my heart sinking. *Though we all will miss him.*

"Well...tomorrow we can examine all this again, I suppose," Miles said. "You need your rest."

"As do you," I said.

He smirked. "That is if I can even fall asleep at this point."

"You should try," I said.

"I will," he said. "You do need to go to bed, though."

"Very well," I said. "Tomorrow we will start this in earnest. I will help."

"I know you will," he said, smiling.

He bid me goodnight before closing the door to his

room, and as I walked back to my own room, I could not help but feel as if I had detected a note of reservation in his voice, or seen a glimmer of doubt in his gaze.

*I fear he is still keeping something from me...*I thought as I settled myself into bed. I tried not to allow my mind to wander to all the possibilities as I drifted off into a fitful sleep filled with uneasy and mysterious sorts of dreams.

7

I woke to a rapping of knuckles against my door.

*Go away...*I thought, my mind still clinging to the fading images of a stroll along Central Park, with a pair of bottle green eyes watching me and laughter filling the air.

"Miss Sylvia?"

I groaned into my pillow and adjusted myself onto my side. Sunlight pierced through the gap between the curtains, begging to be let inside. I blinked, eyes blurry.

"Who-s it?" I managed to mumble through dry lips.

"It's Angelica, Miss. My lady is wondering after you, as you did not appear for breakfast."

It only took a moment before her words sunk in, and I sat up straight in the bed. "What time is it?" I asked, my mind a great deal clearer than it had been.

"A quarter to ten, Miss," the maid answered.

I shifted my legs to the side of the bed, rubbing my eyes. I glanced at the small clock on the bedside table. She was right. "Oh, I – " I said, combing my hair with my fingers as I padded over to the door. I opened it, and found the smiling, anxious face of one of Elizabeth's personal maids waiting on the other side.

"I am terribly sorry," I said. "Please, inform her that all is well. I suppose the travel has finally begun to catch up with me." *Not to mention late night discussions with Miles in his room after midnight*...I mused.

She ducked her head in a curtsy. "Of course, Miss. Shall I send some breakfast up to you?" she asked.

"That would be wonderful, thank you," I said, reaching for my robe hanging on the back of the door. "Pardon me, but where is Miss Elizabeth right now?"

"Down in the parlor, Miss," Angelica answered. Her small lips turned into another smile. "She has taken to writing up thank you notes for the gifts she and Mr. Walton have already received for the wedding."

"Of course," I said, tugging the robe over my night-dress. "Please, will you tell her that I shall be down as soon as I am dressed and ready?"

"Certainly, Miss," she said warmly, curtsying once more before she departed down the hall.

I closed the door, and sagged against it. I laid my head in my hand, feeling for signs of fever. How could I have slept so late? We had been here for three days, and I had yet to default to my usual sleeping patterns. I had not struggled with it at all yet.

I wandered toward my trunk, digging through the contents for something to wear that was not tremendously wrinkled. I settled on an olive green dress and a pair of simple black pumps before beginning to pull them on.

I turned to the mirror where I meant to use the reflection to tie up the ribbons behind my back, when I noticed a note tucked into the frame. Eyes narrowing, I made my way to it and plucked it from its hiding spot.

Unfolding it, my heart sank as I recognized the handwriting immediately, having seen it strewn about my father's office in the last few months with reminders and dates and scheduling.

Dear Miss Sylvia,

First and foremost, I apologize that this is the correspondence that we are to have this morning. It was not my intention to leave it for you, but when I came in to see you this morning, you slept so peacefully that it would have been a travesty to wake you. Your words from last night lingered on my mind, reminding me that our time here in the city is short, and I must be to work. I realize that in light of our agreement to work together, this might be unexpected but I assure you that I have not gone back on what we agreed.

I am off already in the early hours, having been unable

to sleep even a wink last night. I do not suppose I will rest properly until this matter has been resolved in its entirety. I intend to find a way to get to my cousin's estate without him becoming aware, and as such, shall need to do some reconnaissance. I must place myself in a position where I will certainly rub shoulders with the sorts of men who would be bound to notice any beautiful young lady accompanying me. I am sure you understand that I cannot afford the sort of attention that would draw.

I do not plan to be gone terribly long, but I did not think it right for me to leave and not tell you where I was. In the case of your friend, feel free to make what excuses you wish, though perhaps the most believable story, and perhaps the most accurate, is that I have gone to visit my family.

Do take care of yourself, all right? And do not do anything that I would not. I shall see you again soon... though I suppose not soon enough for either of us.

Miles

I bristled at first, feeling betrayed after what we had discussed the night before. Could he not have woken me and taken me along with him? Why would he not allow me to be the eyes and ears that he could not be for the time being.

And yet, as much as I disliked it, his reasoning was sound. If he planned to infiltrate some sort of underbelly of the city, then my presence would only be a hindrance to him. As he had spent time traversing those parts in New York before I had managed to find him, I knew that I did not have to worry about his safety. Still, I disliked the very thought of him having to navigate those sorts of paths to find the answers he so desperately wanted. It did not seem fair, given the truth that he and I both knew.

I sighed, tucking his letter inside the book on my side table. There was nothing I could do now to change his mind. He had already gone.

He will return soon enough, I thought. *Then I shall be able to find a way in which I can help him. Perhaps even by then I shall have come up with an idea that I can share with him.*

I finished dressing, and after running a quick comb through my hair, I hurried down the stairs to meet Elizabeth in the parlor.

"Good morning, dear friend," she crooned at me as I walked in. "My, my, I wondered when the exhaustion would catch up with you. I could hardly believe how much help you have given me after so much traveling."

"I am terribly sorry," I said, taking the seat beside hers at the round table tucked away in the corner. She had a stack of hand painted cards and envelopes of matching size that she seemed about halfway through. "I cannot remember the last time I slept in as late as I have."

"Think nothing of it," she said with a dismissive wave of the pen in her hand. "I have busied myself with thank you cards this morning. You needed the rest. How could I possibly have denied you that when your friend spent most of the day yesterday held up in the same manner?"

*Right...*I thought. "Well...thank you," I said. "I suppose I did need it."

"You more than needed it," she said, her smile only growing. "Here, will you help me seal these envelopes?"

"Of course," I said.

A knock at the door drew both our attentions. It was Angelica.

"I hope you will not mind that I have taken the liberty of having your meal delivered in here with Miss Elizabeth," she said, and another servant hurried into the room with a tray laden with all sorts of delicious treats, most of which were leftover from the party the night before.

"Oh, not at all," I said. "I should have thought it through better before asking you to deliver it to my room. Thank you."

The servants bowed themselves from the room, and Elizabeth eyed the tray. "Well, go on, then," she said. "Eat up."

I could not deny that my stomach ached with hunger, despite having eaten my fill and then some the night before. I did not hesitate to dig into the potato leek soup, nor the crusty rolls that had been slathered with butter just as they had come out of the oven.

"I did see your friend this morning," she said. "He wanted me to tell you he was sorry that he had to leave before you woke, but he intended to go and see his family for part of the day."

"Yes, he left me a note as well," I said.

She nodded. "I am glad he is finally going out to see them. I have enjoyed his company, of course, but I know the real reason for his trip was so he could see his family, as well."

"Yes, exactly," I said.

"And I really should thank you for entertaining my guests last night on my behalf," Elizabeth went on. "So many of them enjoyed speaking with you, and it gave them a chance to have someone to speak with when Peter and I were otherwise occupied."

"It was my pleasure," I said. "I heard some very interesting things last night."

"Oh, I am certain you did," she said, handing me another handful of finished thank you cards for me to fold up and seal. "Any worth sharing?"

"Well..." I said, and hesitated. Would it not be too obvious to ask? No, it would only appear obvious to anyone who knew Miles' connection with the Beechwood name. "I heard about an exclusive party from your cousin, at the manor home of a Beechwood family?"

"Oh," Elizabeth said, looking up from her note to look at me. "That is interesting. Yes, I have heard of this party, but Victoria is right, it is entirely exclusive and not worth worrying over. No one I have ever known has been invited, and so, I cannot tell you a great deal about it."

"Oh...I see," I said. "It sounded rather interesting, especially as it happens to fall this weekend."

"And?" Elizabeth asked. "Why does that matter? Did you assume that we could get an invitation?"

"N – No," I said. "I know how difficult that would be."

"It seems strange that you of all people would be interested in a pretentious party like that one," she said. "What about it tempted you?"

I tried to swallow, dropping my eyes to the envelope in my hand. I should have been more careful about how I had asked about the party. Perhaps been a bit more subtle. "It sounded interesting, that's all. Your cousin made it sound so enjoyable."

"Did she?" Elizabeth asked. She set her pen down and regarded me with a pointed stare. "Sylvia...what are you not telling me?"

"Nothing," I said, far too quickly. "Nothing at all."

"Uh, huh..." she said, raising an eyebrow. "Why am I having a hard time believing you?"

"I don't know what you mean," I said. "These thank you cards look wonderful, by the way. Did you paint them yourself – "

Elizabeth reached over and lowered the envelopes

with a curled pointer finger like the hook of a fishing rod. She still wore an arched brow, and drummed said finger on the stack of envelopes. "Sylvia, you have been acting rather strange since the pair of you arrived," she said in a flat tone. "I have known you for years, and thought it might have something to do with this new butler of yours. Now, I am beginning to think there is something else at work."

Has it truly been that easy to see through me and my actions? I wondered. "Everything is fine," I said. "Truly. You need not worry."

"And yet, for some reason, those words do little to bring me comfort," she said. "Honestly, I cannot imagine that you would want to lie to me. Have I done something not to earn your trust?"

Her words stung, though I didn't think she intended them to be unnecessarily hurtful. I had never had reason not to trust her in the past, so in her mind, it made little sense that I would not want to share with her. If she knew the depth of what I was keeping from her, perhaps she would not question me...

I let out a long, slow breath. "You are perceptive, my friend," I said. "But you must believe me when I say there are some things that are better left unsaid."

Elizabeth's expression did not change.

"Truly," I said, my nerves beginning to hum. "Apart from that, it is not my story to share, so therefore, I cannot tell you."

Still, she did not seem convinced. "Not your story to share..." she said. "So then it must be about Miles."

I cleared my throat and looked away. "I – I – "

"You are a bad liar, is what you are," she said, taking the sealed envelopes and setting them aside. She folded her arms and looked hard at me. "Truly, how have you solved all the cases you have without having developed more skill in deception?"

"I have managed," I said. "Those people do not know me quite as well as you, though."

"So, then I am right?" she asked. "This does have to do with Miles?"

"Elizabeth, you must understand that I am simply not at liberty to say what I know. If I did..." I hesitated.

"If you did, then what?" she asked. "Would Miles be angry if you told me?"

"He most certainly would be," I said. "But more importantly, it could put him in a great deal of danger."

"Why is that?" Elizabeth asked. Her tone shifted from one of annoyance to one of concern.

"He already is in danger," I said.

"He is? How so?" she asked.

I was digging myself into a deeper and deeper hole with every word I spoke. I looked away, my mind trying desperately to come up with a plan as quickly as possible. In truth, I knew that I could trust Elizabeth. If she knew everything, she would not turn on Miles. In fact, she would want to help.

...And perhaps she could help, I thought. *She would have connections in town that neither Miles nor I would know. That could be advantageous...*

But Miles would never forgive me if I told her what had happened, who he really was.

"Perhaps I could help you," Elizabeth said.

"That is something I have considered," I said. "But I really do not believe he would take kindly to me telling you."

"Would you have to tell him?" she asked.

"You have already observed that I am a terrible liar," I said. "He would see right through me."

"If this could help him, then would it not be best to have as much assistance as possible?" she asked. "Especially if he is in danger, as you said?"

I studied her, weighing the options. If I told her, and if she told anyone else, it could put our entire investigation in jeopardy.

However...

Miles was entirely too close to the whole affair. Considering that the murder victim had been his wife, it was unavoidable that he should be so. Yet, I worried that his feelings might lead him into taking rash actions that would actually harm his chances to find the clues he needed. He had already begun to take risks that he normally would not.

I sighed, shaking my head.

"Very well," I said, resigning myself. "I am going

against what I know Miles would want...but I think you might be right. You may be able to help us. Having more help could really mean we could solve this problem sooner, without anyone getting hurt."

Her eyes widened, and she glanced toward the door. "You know that you can trust me, right?" she asked.

"I do," I said. "Which is the only reason I have considered telling you in the first place. I should warn you...what I have to tell you is rather disturbing, and may well change your perception of Miles."

Her expression softened, and she shook her head. "Nothing could change my opinion there," she said. "You think well of him, and I have faith in your judgment."

I looked her straight in the eye, and the surprise in her gaze told me she was beginning to understand.

"...Even if he was accused of murder?" I asked.

8

Elizabeth regarded me with a long, hard stare. Her usual smile had faded, only to be replaced with a frown that did not suit her pretty features. She blinked a time or two before leaning in closer to me.

"You chose your words carefully," she said. "I imagine that is because he did not truly kill anyone?"

My head tilted as I gazed upon her with a renewed appreciation. "That is what you took from what I said?" I asked.

"Well, yes," she said, somewhat annoyed. "Did you assume I would have balked at your statement? Fled in horror? Demanded that you and he leave at once?"

"I did not know what you might do," I admitted. "I certainly did not expect you to take it as well as you have."

She straightened, elevating her chin. "You said that he had been accused of murder, not that he had committed murder," she said, folding her arms. "Anyone with a lick of sense would have realized what that meant."

"So, you believe me?" I asked.

"Why in the world would I have reason not to believe you?" she asked, furrowing her brow at me. "You have never proven yourself untrustworthy, and if you believe that he has not done anything, then I would be a fool to ignore your belief."

"You are a good friend, Elizabeth, and far too kind," I said.

"Yes, well...I can understand now why you were reluctant to tell me," she said, leaning back in her seat. "Murder is not a light matter, is it?"

"Anything but," I finished for her with a sigh.

"How did this happen?" she asked. "Did he come out and tell you?"

"No," I said. "I learned the truth for myself and then confronted him about it."

"How?" she asked.

"Well..." I said. "I suppose I should start at the beginning of this whole mess. I told you about how my uncle was killed, yes? Well, the night he died, amidst the chaos, I ran outside and bumped into Miles. I was chasing after someone I had seen fleeing the building, trying to catch a glimpse of the man, and Miles happened to be standing out in the alleyway. I thought him no more than a vagrant, yet he took off after the man without question. He surprised me with his charming demeanor and well-spoken manner. Moreover, he was obviously a person with very useful skills. In a fit of insanity, I invited him to work for my family."

"And so that is how all that happened," she said. "I had wanted to ask, but had not yet gotten around to it."

"Indeed," I said. "I quickly learned that he had a keen eye for finding information, and as such, after hiring him as our butler, I put him to work helping me find the man who killed my uncle."

"That is truly fascinating," she said, eyes widening. "What in the world are the chances?"

There was a knock at the door, and my heart leapt into my throat.

A servant peered into the room. "My lady? Would you and Miss Sylvia care for some tea before lunch?"

"Thank you, William, that would be fine," she said.

He pushed the door open and carried an already prepared tray to us, setting it down on the table beside us. He lifted the teapot, and with great care, he filled each cup for us.

My heart pounded in my ears. Had he heard part of our conversation? How long was he standing outside the door? I should have been wiser. I never should have shared this information with Elizabeth. That lapse of judgment could very well have ruined everything –

"Miss?"

I looked up.

"Would you care for sugar?"

"Oh, yes, please," I said.

He smiled at me and placed a few lumps in my cup, agonizingly slowly.

I resisted the urge to drum my fingers against the table as he poured a slow splash of milk into each cup. He then set down the creamer, bowed, and left the room.

I blew out the air gathered in my cheeks.

"What's the matter?" Elizabeth asked, lifting the tea to sip.

"I worried that he overheard us..." I said.

She shook her head, blowing on the steaming tea. "Do not worry. William is a timid boy, and always working hard. If he was outside the room for more than a moment, I would be surprised."

"Are you sure?" I asked.

She smiled. "Relax, dear friend. He is trustworthy. He may as well be a mouse, as skittish and frightened as he often is. Jumps at his own shadow."

"If you are sure..." I said. "I never thought I would be so paranoid."

"Well, given what you are looking into..." she said. She gave me a nod. "Go on, then. Finish your tale. I should like to learn how you found all this out about Miles."

"Very well," I said. "Let's see, where did I leave off... Well, after he moved in and we solved the mystery of my uncle's death, I was helping move him to his designated room. We had first put him up in a guest room, and then moved him to a room that was prepared for him properly. As I carried his things, I happened to drop a book that fell open. Inside was a newspaper clipping, along with a photo. It was someone who looked like him with a young woman, and the title of the article was something akin to *Husband murders his wife in Hyde Park.* Or some such."

Elizabeth gasped. "This is why you asked me about that in the letter!" she exclaimed. "I wondered why you asked about it out of the blue. Now it is all beginning to make sense."

"I dismissed a lot of my suspicion at first, given his character did not seem that of a murderer, but then more clues continued to appear, such as my catching him throwing something into the river to dispose of it, and my finding out not long after that it was a gun."

"A gun?" Elizabeth repeated.

"The murder weapon, no less," I said. "And I managed to have a fisherman fish it out of the depths."

"My word..." Elizabeth said. "That certainly does seem incriminating."

"I only had pieces of the puzzle by that point," I

said. "And my assumptions. Unfortunately, all signs at that time suggested Miles was the one to have killed her."

Elizabeth shook her head. "It seems that whoever did kill the woman did an excellent job of making Miles appear guilty," she said.

"Precisely," I said. "For it was not until I confronted him about it myself that he told me the truth."

"Even he must have known that the evidence was not in his favor," Elizabeth said.

"Yes," I said. "That is precisely the trouble, isn't it? He said as much to me. At first, he did not want to tell me. In a way, I think he had resigned himself to his fate. He did not see a way out apart from some sort of miracle."

"How did you manage to convince him to tell you what happened?" Elizabeth asked.

"He realized that he had no choice but to tell me when I confronted him. My sister went missing during that time, and it was not until after we had worked together to find her that we were able to sit down and speak of it once more."

"I see…" Elizabeth said. "And what did he tell you?"

"He told me he was not at all who he seemed," I said. "That he was, in fact, a wealthy man who had been forced to flee London when he was framed for his late wife's murder."

"His wife?" Elizabeth repeated, eyes widening.

"Yes," I said.

"Well, who killed her?" Elizabeth asked. "Did he ever find out?"

"He is almost certain," I said. "His cousin...Felton Beechwood."

Her mouth formed a small *O*, and understanding shone in her eyes. "I knew there was a reason you were so interested in that place," she said. "I assume the pair of you wish to go to find more clues to prove Miles' innocence?"

"Miles has no idea about the party," I said, a twinge of guilt knotting in my gut. "And he would be recognized by his cousin the moment he laid eyes on him."

"True..." Elizabeth said. She brightened. "Is that why he would not come down to our party last night?"

"Yes," I said. "He felt dreadful about it, but he could not risk anyone seeing him that would recognize him."

"No one knows he is innocent," Elizabeth said. "And there would surely be people in town who would recognize him, not to mention those who might leap at the chance to telephone the police and tell them they've spotted a wanted criminal."

"Precisely," I said. "He has taken to going out at night to find information under the cover of darkness."

"Clever," Elizabeth said. "And has he yet been successful?"

"Not as far as I know," I said. "All he knows is that his cousin is suspicious, paranoid that he might be being followed. Miles wonders if his cousin guesses that he has returned to London to seek vengeance."

"Well, he would not be wrong about that, would he?" she asked.

"Right..." I said. "Which leads me to apologize to you. I hope you know that I did wish to come visit so that I might see you before the wedding, but our main motive for coming was so that we might investigate and clear Miles' name. I am sorry, my friend, for having mislead you."

"Oh, my dear Sylvia," Elizabeth said, reaching over and taking both my hands in hers. "You need not apologize! This is a noble effort and I am elated I could be of help to you and Miles!"

"Really?" I asked. "You are not angry with me?"

"How could I be?" she asked. "You are here, are you not? I don't suppose that because you wanted to help Miles that you love me any less. If anything, it still allowed us to be together, did it not?"

"I...suppose it did, yes," I said.

"Perhaps, now you can have more help," Elizabeth said. "With more heads working together, we are sure to find a way to get Miles out of this mess."

"That was my hope," I said. "But I should warn you...these sorts of investigations can become complicated."

"Need I remind you that we took Logic together in school?" she asked.

"I certainly remember," I said. "You were the top of our class."

"Indeed I was," she said, a smile growing on her face. "And I still have been fascinated with the subject. I read about logic a great deal, and my Peter refuses to play chess with me any longer as I beat him mercilessly every time."

I smiled. "It seems that you have only gotten better, then. You did manage to deduce that I was hiding something from you."

"Exactly," she said with a nod. "And so what are the next steps? How can I help?"

"That is where I am struggling," I said. "Miles is concerned about me being involved, fearing that he is putting me in danger."

Her brow furrowed. "But have you not been conducting these sorts of investigations for some time now?" she asked. "Having been in danger before?"

"Indeed," I said. "But he feels this is his responsibility."

"Yes, but no one knows you here in London," Elizabeth said. "You could be vital in learning the truth, even more so than myself."

"That is my point precisely," I said. "I have said the same to him, but he does not want me to be at the forefront of the whole affair."

"That is understandable, given that he cares so much for you," she said.

I opened my mouth to protest, but she went on.

"There really is no use in continuing to deny your care for him, either," she chided me, arching a brow at me. "You do not like that he is taking risks, yes? Do not like that he is myopic about finding his clues? Well, then you should consider how allowing those sorts of feelings may put you both in danger, unchecked as they are."

"I – " I said, but my cheeks flushed scarlet. "How can I? He is our – "

"Butler, yes, you keep saying," Elizabeth said. "But that isn't true, is it? Not any longer. You and he would be of equal standing."

"He is still in love with his wife," I said.

Elizabeth glared at me. "Has he said that?"

"How could he not be?" I asked. "She was taken away from him, after they had only been married a short time. And he told me how enamored they were with one another..."

"He cannot bring her back," Elizabeth said. "Not to sound all together heartless, but there is nothing he can do about her now. If he wishes, he could spend the rest of his life alone. I think he has realized that it would be far better for him to move past it and try to find joy once again. He certainly seems to be happy when he is with you."

I sighed, losing the will to argue with her.

"All I am saying is that you should not waste a great

deal of time before telling one another how you feel," she said. "The both of you. Please, just consider what I am saying."

"I will..." I said.

"But your trouble now is this weekend party," Elizabeth said.

I straightened in my seat. "Yes. It is the best chance I have to find information right within his cousin's residence."

"That makes sense," she said.

"So how might I get an invitation?" I asked.

"It will be tricky, but we may be able to use your anonymity to your advantage," she said. "I will need to speak with Peter to come up with a proper plan – "

"Elizabeth, I do not know if it would be wise to let anyone else know about Miles," I said.

"Yes, but you must understand that Peter will be of great use," she said. "And trust me...you can trust him."

I had already accepted the fact that Miles would be displeased with me for telling Elizabeth. "What is the harm, I suppose?" I asked. "As long as we can be sure that he will not speak a word of it to anyone."

"He will not," Elizabeth said. "You have my word."

For now that would have to suffice. I had already come this far.

9

"You mean to tell me..." Mr. Walton said, looking back and forth between Elizabeth and I. "That you have been housing a wanted criminal?"

"You make it sound so terrible," Elizabeth said.

"I'm sorry," Mr. Walton said, looking at me. "I do not mean to belittle Miles. I rather like the fellow. But are you really quite sure this is safe? For Elizabeth and her family, I mean?"

"You were quick to believe me," I said. "Which is a relief."

"I told you he would," Elizabeth said. "See? You had nothing to worry about."

"I did not truly fear that I did," I said. "And Elizabeth and her family are perfectly safe. Miles and I have gone to great lengths to ensure that he is not recognized. You can rest assured that he will make sure that he is not ever followed, nor will he attract the wrong sort of attention." I sighed. "Which is part of the reason why I fear that he will never find the answers he seeks."

"Which is why you have enlisted our help," Mr. Walton said. He drew in a deep, steadying breath. "I can understand your situation. It must be quite difficult not to know whether he will ever be able to leave behind these shackles that bind him."

"We are hoping to help him do just that," I said.

"Which is why we need your help, darling," Elizabeth said, snaking her arm beneath his.

"Yes, I see," he said. "Sylvia, I must stress that I only will allow my dear Elizabeth to be involved in all this if I am involved as well."

"That makes a great deal of sense," I said. "And I shall honor that request...as long as you can assure me that no one else outside of we three will learn Miles' identity."

He looked down at his plate of treacle tarts that he had ordered from the bakery that we had gone to in order to speak. This late in the afternoon, we practically had the entire place to ourselves. Elizabeth had chosen a cozy little table in the back corner of the room, tucked between a pair of bookshelves housing old, musty books. A candle burned low in a small, glass votive in the center of us all, casting long shadows along the table.

"I assure you, I will not tell another soul," he said. "I understand how important this is. Justice must be done, and I will do my part to help you and Miles. Keeping his secret is the least that I can do and should not be difficult to accomplish."

"Thank you," I said.

"Now, my dear, will you be able to help Sylvia to get an invitation to this party at the home of Felton Beechwood?" Elizabeth asked.

"It is going to be difficult," he said. "The Beechwood family has a tight social circle, and they are not often looking for reasons to widen it. There is...one way that I can think of, though."

"Which is what?" I asked.

"It would be to befriend his mistress, Miss Colette," he said. "I am familiar with her, at least in passing, as she is a regular frequenter of a particular teahouse that I often visit."

I straightened, my heart skipping a few beats. "Truly?" I asked. "That is better news than I could have expected. I would have thought we would have to jump through a myriad of hoops just to find a connection."

"Do not mistake what I am saying," Mr. Walton said. "The owner of the teahouse is my own cousin, but I have heard that Miss Colette is quite difficult to impress. She only wishes to surround herself with the most important and interesting people."

Elizabeth looked over at me. "That might work."

"How?" I asked. "There is nothing terribly interesting about me, nor important."

"Why don't we see if I can manage to secure you a table at the teahouse when Miss Colette is meant to be there next," Mr. Walton said, getting up from the table. "I may well be able to do so within the next day or two."

Two days... Who knows what danger might befall Miles in that time. "Very well," I said aloud, trying to appear positive and encouraged. "I appreciate you going to such lengths, Mr. Walton."

Mr. Walton telephoned Elizabeth just before dinner that evening. When she returned to the parlor that we had been sitting in together, she wore a broad smile. "I have good news," she said, resuming her seat across from me at the chess set. "Peter convinced his cousin to find a place for us at Miss Colette's table at the teahouse."

"When?" I asked.

"Sooner than expected. This evening, at seven," Elizabeth said, her eyes alight. "I hope you are ready."

"As ready as I will be," I said. I glanced up at the

clock, seeing that we had a little over an hour to dress and leave for the teahouse. *Miles has not come back yet today...*I thought. *I hope he is all right...*

"What should we wear?" I asked. "I have never been to a proper teahouse in London before."

"It's a rather involved affair," she said. "Do not worry, I will ensure you are ready."

I went with her upstairs where she looked through my trunk and found a dress of a deep rose color with gold sequins forming a sunburst pattern down the front. She paired it with her necklace once again, and some of my best shoes. "You must treat this as a real occasion," she said. "But know that your attire will only be judged by the other women in attendance."

I smirked at her as I pinned some curls away from my face. "Is that not how social events always are?" I asked.

"You are not wrong, my friend," she said.

We sent for the car, and headed out to the teahouse a short while later. My palms grew slick as we drove along. I had little idea what to expect. I knew that no one would recognize me. No one had any reason to even know who I was. But I knew them, and knew who this Miss Colette was involved with. I wondered if she was aware of what he had done, that he had killed a woman so that he might inherit his cousin's wealth...

UPON MEETING MISS COLETTE, I quickly realized that Felton Beechwood could have been the devil himself and she likely would not have cared.

She had hair as fine as silk, as dark as if it had been dyed with ink. She had pointed, thin features and full lips. It was easy to see why a man would be immediately smitten with her, yet at the same time why she would repulse any number of women around who could see her for what she was; a menace.

We heard her before we saw her. She cackled as she strode into the teahouse, flanked by a trio of other pretty women, though each was less so than herself. I assumed she did that purposely so that she would always be the center of attention.

Mr. Walton's cousin, the proprietor of the teahouse, welcomed Miss Colette and her group inside, bringing them to the table that she had already seated us at.

Miss Colette did not bother to thank her, instead her gaze falling upon us, eyes flashing. "Pardon me, but have we met?" she asked.

I did my best to wear my most innocent smile. "I do not believe we have," I said.

Miss Colette folded her arms, her body undulating with annoyance. "An American?" she asked, a smirk growing. "My, my. What a rare treat."

Despite the sarcasm, a glint in her eyes told me I had her full attention.

Maybe Elizabeth is right. Maybe this will work.

"My name is Miss Shipman," I said. I had debated about using my real name, but on the off chance that she recognized it, I knew I had to use it. "Would you please join us for tea this evening?"

Perhaps it was my confidence that won her over and convinced her that I was worth talking to, for I sensed she was impressed, in spite of herself.

"You must be rather important, if our hostess seated you with us," Miss Colette said, sliding into the chair directly across from me. She moved lithely, laying her chin against the back of her hand, swaying like a serpent in a trance. She completely ignored her companions, who quietly drew up seats nearby. "How *very* interesting. What business is your family in, Miss Shipman?"

"My father is in finance," I said. "Spends a great deal of time with the stock market."

Miss Colette raised an eyebrow. "Finance, you say?" she asked. "Then you and I will understand one another quite well. My father is in banking."

"Indeed?" I asked. "Then I suppose we would have crossed paths, if you and your family were in New York."

She smirked again. "You're quite funny. New York, you say?"

"Yes, we live in the city," I said. "Though I am now finding the quaint charm of London to be quite to my liking."

"Well, how pleased I am to hear it," Miss Colette said. "I have never been to New York, but have always wanted to go. Is it as modern and sophisticated as I have heard?"

"Even more so," I said. "The city is incredibly bright at all hours of the day. There are theaters galore, jazz clubs, restaurants, parties to attend... Few places I have ever been are quite as glamorous."

"How exciting..." Miss Colette said, her eyes shining. "London can be such a bore. Is it true that you can enjoy food from all over the world?"

"We have markets from almost every corner of the globe," I said. "My particular favorite has become the Italian bakeries that are near our family home. Filled with cream, flaky, buttery – "

"Oh, come now, Miss Shipman, you will make us all ravenous," Miss Colette said.

I glanced sidelong at Elizabeth, who gave me an encouraging nod. It was better if I did not draw any attention to her. If she remained quiet, Miss Colette may well think she was nothing more than my servant or some such.

"Mrs. Barnabas, we are ready for our tea," Miss Colette said.

Mr. Walton's cousin came to the table, pushing a cart with a beautiful, painted teapot and matching cups and saucers.

"This is my particular favorite blend," Miss Colette said. "Rather spicy, but it is bright and light."

"Sounds akin to some of the Moroccan tea that my father imported," I said.

"I love Moroccan tea," Miss Colette said, her eyes growing wide. "When I am able to get my hands on any of it."

That might have been a bit of a stretch, as I had only ever heard Joan speak of such tea. I never had the chance to try it, myself. It was good, as I sipped it gently. I made sure to take it black, just as Miss Colette did. Bitter on my tongue, but refreshing. I would have preferred some milk to cut through the spiciness, but I wanted to give her yet another reason to like me. It might have been small, but it could make the difference.

"Tell me, Miss Shipman, have you been enjoying your time in London thus far? Has it held up to your standards in entertainment?" Miss Colette asked as Mrs. Barnabas delivered a tray of lace tea cookies to our table.

"I suppose..." I said, flippant, taking a proffered cookie. "There may not be as much excitement as I am used to at home, but I am enjoying my time for the most part."

"Well..." she said, smirking at me, head swaying like a snake once again. "I really think that you should come and visit this weekend, so you might be shown proper London entertainment."

That she would bring it up herself so early in the conversation seemed almost too easy. Could it be a trap? But why should it be? She could not possibly suspect our plan...

I considered, glancing at Elizabeth. I could see the excitement alight in Elizabeth's gaze.

As lazily as I could, I looked back at Miss Colette. "I suppose something could be arranged," I said. "Would you care if my cousin were to come along with me? I can only see her once every few years, and this trip was meant to be our time together."

"Absolutely," Miss Colette said with a laugh and shrug of her shoulders. "The more people, the merrier our time shall be."

I grinned at her, my hands shaking slightly beneath the table. "Wonderful," I said. "I greatly look forward to it."

10

I could not have been more pleased with myself.

I had gone into the teahouse without any expectations. I had wondered what Miss Colette would be like, and to consider her simple would have been a kindness. Not only had I realized that she was not the sort of person I would usually associate myself with, but she also made herself far too easy to read.

"I suppose she never has had reason to suspect people," Elizabeth said when I voiced that thought to her. "No troubles, in that regard."

"It almost seemed too easy to get her to believe what I wanted," I said. "I will have to be careful that she does not see through that during our time with them."

"I don't believe you will have to worry," Elizabeth

said. "Your role was well played. You even made me question how well I knew you."

I smirked at her as we headed back to the car waiting to take us home.

It was a short drive back to the house, and we rode in silence, each of us likely lost in our own thoughts.

"How did it go?" Mr. Walton asked after we arrived back at the house. He had come to meet us there, his face lacking much color.

"Incredibly well," Elizabeth said, beaming at him. "She got an invitation!"

Mr. Walton looked at me, his eyes widening. "You did?" he asked. "How?"

"She found me funny," I said with a shrug. "And her family is in banking. My father is in finance. Apparently, that makes us equals. Or at least similar."

"My word," Mr. Walton said. "And she had no idea that you were attempting to hoodwink her?"

"Not as far as I could tell," I said. "I did not even have to ask for an invitation. She offered it to me."

His brow furrowed. "And you are sure she is not aware of who you are? What if this is a trap?"

A small trickle of fear ran down my spine. Hadn't I thought the same myself? "You are right to wonder," I said. "That has crossed my mind as well, and I intend to be careful."

"I understand your worry, my dear," Elizabeth said to her fiancé. "But that woman is a simpleton. I doubt she can remember what she had for breakfast. All she seems to care about is her own image and those who might entertain her. Sylvia fit that mold this time, but I cannot imagine that she will have had any malicious intent. She sways with the whims of her friends, and I imagine she never lets a night pass without some sort of shallow social function or gathering. It seems to be all she cares about."

"That certainly does seem to be her primary care in life," I said.

"Yes, but what if Miles' cousin, told her to invite... well, no, that would not make any sense, would it?" Mr. Walton asked. "He wouldn't have had any idea you were going there tonight. Besides, that would assume he knew of the connection between you and Miles in the first place. And unless he is incredibly clever and able to think that far ahead, anticipating so many actions..."

Miles is clever, so it is not all together difficult to imagine that someone he is related to would be as well, I thought with a growing sense of dread. *Nevertheless, I still think it is almost impossible that someone would be able to pair Miles and me together, especially as Miles has not been using his real name for the time being.* I had to keep reminding myself that Miles was nothing more than a nickname, something he had taken when coming to New York to help him hide.

"Speaking of Miles," Mr. Walton said, waving us

into the parlor off the foyer. "He came home for a brief time, but has already taken off again."

My heart sank as I followed him and Elizabeth. "He did?"

"He did, but he wrote up a note for you before he left," Mr. Walton said, turning around to pass me a folded piece of paper.

I took it without saying anything, and quickly unfolded it.

I am terribly sorry to have to do this, but I cannot wait any longer. I hoped that you would return before I had to leave, but a lead that I believe I have found is far too promising for me to pass up. I am going to go and pursue it. I will explain the details later. I may not return for a day or two. Be safe.

I sighed, my hand and the note in it falling to my side.

"Is everything all right?" Elizabeth asked.

I shook my head. "It is hard to say. He is leaving for a few days."

"Leaving?" Elizabeth asked.

"To go where?" Mr. Walton asked.

"I have no clue," I said. "All he said is that he might have found a lead, and he intends to pursue it."

"Well...that could be good, couldn't it?" Elizabeth asked. "If it would help lead him to answers?"

"Yes, but he may end up being wrong," I said. "He didn't explain what he is doing or where he is going." I frowned. "It is not like him to hide that sort of information from me."

"Is he hiding it?" she asked. "Or is he not even thinking of telling you in the first place because he is so caught up in his own thoughts?"

"Perhaps..." I said. "And he might have worried about putting anything in the note that might be read by someone other than me. He is trying to cover his tracks, and by doing so, becoming horribly paranoid. No one here would betray him." *Though maybe he would say that I was betraying him for telling Elizabeth and Mr. Walton in the first place...*I thought.

I looked at Elizabeth. "He has no idea that I have told either of you. If he did..." I trailed off. There was no need to think of that, for it would likely be days now before he learned that I had told them. "But perhaps this is for the best," I went on. "It will give us the chance to go away for the weekend without him ever having to know, and when we reconvene, we can perhaps both share any facts we have learned that could clear his name."

"That's the spirit," Elizabeth said. "He will forgive you, if that is what you are concerned about."

I nodded. This was my helping, I knew that. I could get into his cousin's home, undetected, and snoop around in a way that Miles simply could not. Perhaps this would mean that we would find the clues we needed even sooner.

"It is just as well he is gone," Elizabeth went on. "If he were here, he would likely be worrying over you the whole time. He might have protested your going, or even stormed his cousin's house, blowing both his own cover and yours."

"That would be horrendous," I said. "It would spoil everything."

"Precisely," she agreed. "Which is why I do think it will be for the best that he does not know until later. This may well be for his own good."

"I certainly hope so," I said.

"What is the plan, then?" Mr. Walton asked. "When do you intend to leave?"

"Tomorrow, first thing," Elizabeth said. "The party is meant to take place Friday through Sunday, and Miss Colette informed us that we could arrive anytime around noon."

He blinked. "Oh – Oh, I see. Does this mean the both of you are going?" he asked, eyeing Elizabeth in particular. "Do you really suppose that is wise, my dear? Will you not be in danger?"

"I will have Sylvia with me," she said.

"Mr. Walton, I understand your concern," I said. "But you have my word that not a hair on Elizabeth's head will be touched, much less harmed."

"I appreciate your care for her, and I do trust that you will protect her to the very best of your ability," Mr. Walton said. "But would it not be wise for me to perhaps join the pair of you? Not only could I assure that you are both unharmed, which I know would greatly encourage Miles as well, but I could be at ease that while Elizabeth is in the presence of a killer, she is safe."

I sighed, shaking my head. "It would be a relief if you were able to come, except that only Elizabeth and I were invited along. As it was, I worried that I might have been asking too much to allow her to come, even under the guise that she was my cousin."

"Besides, Peter, if you were there, then we would likely not be able to pass through the estate as easily unnoticed," Elizabeth said, taking his hand. "I will miss you dearly, you know I will, and I hate to make you worry." Her eyes brightened, and she gave him a bit of a shake. "Oh, I know! Why don't we make an agreement to speak over the telephone every few hours? I could call you from their estate, and claim lovesickness. Surely, no one will care if I am merely checking in with my fiancé."

"I doubt they would care at all," I said, smiling. "That's a wonderful idea, Elizabeth."

Mr. Walton did not seem so cheered.

"Come now," Elizabeth said. "Would that not comfort you?"

"What would comfort me would be that you remained here, at home," Mr. Walton said.

Elizabeth frowned at him. "You cannot be so terse,

my love. It does not suit you."

He sighed, looking away. "All right," he said. "I suppose I shall swallow my fears and trust you. And you will be in contact every few hours?"

"Why don't we agree on just after breakfast, just after luncheon, before tea...and then after dinner?" she asked.

"That could work," Mr. Walton said. "And what are we to tell your parents?"

"I will speak with them shortly, and I will tell them everything apart from the intent to investigate," Elizabeth said. "They will be pleased and surprised that I managed to secure an invitation, as these parties are rather exclusive."

Mr. Walton glanced at me. "And what of Miles? What will he think when he returns and no one is here to greet him?"

"Do not worry," I said. "I shall leave him a note explaining things, in the event that he does come back before Elizabeth and I do." Though something told me he would not return before us...and that perhaps he might have put himself in danger as well.

I couldn't afford to waste the time worrying over him right now, however. He would be able to take care of himself, just as I must.

"Well...I suppose I shall need to pack up a bag," I said. "I certainly hope I have brought the proper attire with me for this trip."

"Oh, I shall help you," Elizabeth said. "We will have you all suited up to look like the proper socialite that you are."

"I shall leave you ladies to it, then," Mr. Walton said with an incline of his head. "This area is not of my expertise, and I shall only be in your way."

"Do come back for breakfast in the morning, though, won't you, dear?" Elizabeth asked.

He smiled at her, his face warming. "You have my word," he said.

She beamed.

We retired upstairs to pack our suitcases, Elizabeth seeming to be enjoying herself more than I would have expected, considering that we were both going into a potentially dangerous weekend. She went on and on about the dresses she wanted to wear, dresses she wanted me to wear, as if she had forgotten the risks involved in our plan.

"Oh, will you excuse me for a moment?" Elizabeth asked as she pawed through my dresses, half a dozen already tossed out onto the bed to pack. "I would like to pack a particular pair of shoes, and am certain that if I do not go now and fetch them, I will certainly forget them."

"Off you go, then," I said with a laugh.

She darted from the room, humming to herself.

I shook my head, smiling as she left. *Perhaps I should be more lighthearted going into this weekend,* I thought, sitting down at the writing desk in the corner. I liked the idea of being more carefree about the whole affair, but whenever I tried to be, I remembered that I would be face to face with Miles' cousin, the man who had murdered Sophia.

I cannot take this lightly, I told myself. *I must be on my guard at all times. It will not only be my life that I am trying to protect.*

I wished Miles were still here, that he had not run off on me to look after a lead.

But it really would not matter, would it? If he was here, all he would do is argue with me about going in the first place, and possibly try to stop me, for my own safety. If he was here, then I might not be going at all, and we would be exactly where we started.

This truly was the better option, and I knew that I had to take advantage of it...

Still, I wish this was something he and I could go through together. I am used to having his assistance in these matters...

I needed to give him an explanation, just as I told Mr. Walton I would. If he came back tomorrow, he should know where I was, shouldn't he?

Of course, he had not given me the same courtesy, and I had next to no idea where in London he could be at that moment. Nevertheless, I would leave him some information, so that he would not be in the dark as to my plans.

I found a small, blank piece of paper that had only one dog-eared edge, along with a pen and an envelope. My hand shook as I poised the pen over the page, uncertain what to write...and how much to tell him.

Miles

Writing his name even felt strange now, because I knew full well that it might be the name that I knew him by, but it was not his *real* name. Yet I could hardly use any other, could I?

I shook my head. That was another worry for another day.

I debated whether or not to tell you where I was, as I knew that you would be displeased with me once you learned the truth, but Elizabeth and I have gone to your cousin's estate outside of the city for a weekend retreat.

I gazed at the statement, wondering how it would be received. Poorly, I should think.

We managed to secure a personal invitation from his mistress at a teahouse. Do not fear, she has no idea who I am. No one apart from Elizabeth and Mr. Walton have any idea that I have a connection with you. I realize that you will not take kindly to this news, and I have come to terms with it. I know full well that you cannot go out to your cousin's house for risk of being discovered.

When I learned about the party, I knew that I had to take full advantage of it. I would have been a fool not to. I could not sit by idly and wait for you to either get yourself killed or for us to return to New York empty-handed. This is a chance for me to get up close with your cousin, and to look through his personal belongings to find what we are looking for. We may never get another chance like this, and I refuse to go back to New York with you still having to hide behind the name of Miles.

I owe you a great deal. My life, several times over, for one thing. You must allow me to repay the many times you have assisted my family. You must allow me to help you get your life back.

I should be home by Sunday afternoon, or even before that, if I am able to find the evidence that we need. I will be careful. I will ensure that everything goes smoothly. And if I am able, I will bring you the very item that you need to prove your innocence, whatever it may be.

I heard Elizabeth down the hall humming once more, returning to my room.

Say a prayer for me, as I will for you. Let us hope that we are both successful in our endeavors, and can be together once again, safe and sound.

All my heart,

Sylvia

I blanched a bit at the way I had signed the letter, but did not have a chance to change it before Elizabeth twirled into the room, cradling a dress against herself as if she were dancing with a living, breathing human.

I folded the note, some of the ink still damp, before slipping it into the envelope.

"What do you think? This dress with these shoes?

Or perhaps with that violet dress that I wore last night?" she asked. She swung a pair of leather shoes, tied up with navy blue ribbons, from the tips of her fingers.

"I think that dress is quite smart," I said, slipping the letter beneath a hat box she had set down on the writing table just a short while before. "Though is it at all possible that we are packing a bit too much for only two nights away?"

"One can never have too many dresses," Elizabeth said with a firm nod. "Besides, if you are claiming to be a wealthy woman from a prominent family, you should look the part."

"But that's exactly who I am," I pointed out.

"Yes, but you might do well to dress a bit more... luxurious," she said with a grin. "We might as well help you carry on with that nonchalant attitude, yes? I think it will help you fit in with the sorts that we will be surrounding ourselves with this weekend."

"I suppose you are right," I said, getting up to finish packing the clothes she had selected for me. "Regardless of how I might normally dress, it is a good idea that I try to create a bit of a character, as opposed to being entirely myself."

"Precisely," Elizabeth said. "And I shall be your doting cousin who is not fit to kiss your shoes."

I smirked at her. "Oh, is that who you have chosen to play?"

"Indeed," she said with a toss of her hair. "I have come up with a new name, a new place of residence, and a whole new life story."

"That could be useful," I said. "Thank you, Elizabeth, for being willing to help me."

"I am glad to," she said warmly. "Now, have you chosen your shoes? Or hats? Those are just as important as your clothes, in my opinion."

I smiled as the time whiled away as she selected the appropriate accessories for my outfits while I watched. In a way, it reminded me of Joan and how she liked to do the very same. It made me miss her in that moment.

"Are you going to be ready for this?" Elizabeth asked.

"I think so," I said. "This will not be the first time that I have walked into the mouth of the beast."

She nodded, but did not meet my eye.

"And yourself?" I asked.

"I think so," she said. "I suppose I shall have to see if I have enough steel in my spine."

"You will do fine," I said. "I will be there with you. I won't let you out of my sight."

"I know," she said, smiling at me. "Still...I do hope that we won't be in too much danger."

I wished I could promise her we would not, but how could I?

"We will be going in with our eyes wide open," I

said. "We are already aware of the risks before we arrive, and that puts us a great deal ahead of them. Also, I think it is highly unlikely Miles' cousin will do anything to us unless he learns who we are, which I doubt will happen."

"Then I have great confidence in you and your sleuthing ability," she said.

"I will keep you safe, Elizabeth," I said. "I promise you."

She smiled. "I know you will," she said. "Who would have ever thought that we would be putting our skills on the line in such a way?"

"Your ability to think quickly and clearly will help me a great deal," I said. "Your input will be vital on this excursion."

"You are too kind," she said.

"I mean it," I said. "But you really must prepare yourself. When we step into that house, we cannot turn away without appearing suspicious. It will strike you what we are doing when we get there, and by then, it will be too late to turn back."

"I know," she said.

"If you want to change your mind, I will understand," I said.

She shook her head. "No. I will not leave you to do this alone. I will stay with you and help you."

"Very well," I said. "Then let us make sure we get a good night's sleep. Tomorrow will come before we are ready for it."

11

Felton Beechwood's home sat atop a hill outside London, about fifteen miles from the city center, which took hardly any time at all to reach by car. Elizabeth wrung her favorite silk gloves between her hands as we rode. She hardly said a word, but I could understand.

She is frightened, I realized. *And I must admit that I am not all together confident now that we are approaching the house.*

My heart leapt at the sight of every house on the horizon, every driveway that we passed. I knew that I feared meeting Felton, but at the same time, a bizarre, nostalgic longing filled me to see part of Miles' life. It was a sad sort of tug, akin to visiting a suffering relative that one has not seen in years, or witnessing a fight between a couple in a public place. I did not want to believe that he had a whole life before we had crossed paths in New York in that back alley, but at the same time, I didn't want to miss the chance to learn all I could about him.

The whole push and pull twisted my stomach in tight knots, making it difficult to draw deep breaths to try and relax.

I didn't know what sort of afternoon to expect, but I had no idea that we would be greeted by a long row of servants and maids lined up along either side of the drive as we drove up to the manor. As our car came to a stop, they all dipped into curtsies or bowed in unison, bending at the waist, as if they were no more than dolls.

Elizabeth turned a wide pair of eyes on me, her mouth hanging partially open. Was this how Miles had grown up, amid such elegance and formality?

"Do you see the house?" Elizabeth asked. "It makes mine look like a doll's house."

Leaning closer to the car window, I turned my face up at the shining sun, shielded partially by the tower on the southern corner. As I gazed around, I realized that it was one of three towers, one of which was as wide as my family's rowhouse in Sutton Place back in New York.

"I know what you mean..." I said. "It is positively enormous, isn't it?"

"Bigger than almost any I have ever seen," she said.

One of the servants, a middle-aged man approached the car with a polite smile on his face. He reached the back door, and pulled it open.

"Welcome to the Beechwood manor," he said. "Miss Shipman and her cousin, I presume?"

"I am Miss Moon," Elizabeth said, laying her now gloved hand against her chest. She gestured gracefully toward me. "This is Miss Shipman."

"Welcome, to the both of you. If your driver would open the boot, I should be happy to take your bags for you," he said. "Oh, and my name is Mr. Henry, Mr. Beechwood's butler."

"Well, thank you," I said. "We are glad to be here."

He smiled again, as Elizabeth stepped out from the car and I followed her.

The sun shone down, though it lacked warmth. Wind brushed through the branches of the young trees along the side of the house, but apart from the rustling of the leaves, not a sound was heard. Somehow the short distance had swallowed the sounds of the city.

The line of uniformed servants parted as Elizabeth and I started toward the main door to the house, where Mr. Henry led us. We might as well have been the only guests expected. A shiver raced down my spine as I felt their eyes fall upon our backs. These people had no idea who we were, yet they had all quite clearly been prepared for our arrival.

What have they been told about us? I wondered.

"You will have to forgive the sparse greenery, given the time of year," Mr. Henry said. "The summer months are some of the best at the manor, with rose bushes in full bloom, the orchard fruits just beginning to come in, and the back garden welcoming butterflies."

"It is still quite breathtaking," I said.

Mr. Henry smiled at me over his shoulder. "My master will be quite pleased to hear you say so."

He pushed open the front door and stepped aside, allowing us to pass by him.

The foyer beyond resided within one of the towers, wider around than my family's drawing room. A trio of doorways branched out from the tower, but the most impressive part of the room was the large, marble fountain that echoed the circular shape of the tower. The bubbling, sparkling water filled the room with life and movement.

"Oh, *hello* there!"

The voice came from behind the fountain, and a woman with inky black hair appeared around the outside...closely followed by Miles.

My stomach dropped to my feet in surprise, and my knees almost gave out beneath me.

He lifted his chin, his eyes passing over me...

Wait – I thought. *That's not Miles. That must be* –

"Oh, darling, this is *her*, this is who I was telling you

about!" said the dark-haired woman, who was Miss Colette.

Was she talking about me?

She came hurrying over to me, her eyes bright and shining. She threw her arms wide and wrapped them squarely around my neck. "Oh, how pleased I am that you've come. I have been looking forward to this since we met!"

Was that not just last night?

"Colette..." said the man behind her, his hands sliding into his trouser pockets. "Please, do not overwhelm our guests.

I gazed upon him, practically stunned into silence. The two even *sounded* alike.

His mannerisms, the way he moved, even the way he brushed some of that sandy blonde hair from his line of sight...Felton and Miles may well have passed as twins. The greatest difference I could see upon a longer, lingering look told me that Felton might have had a few inches on Miles, but apart from that, it was difficult to tell them apart.

The eyes, though...the eyes are different, yes? I thought quickly as his gaze fell upon me.

Miles had clear green eyes the same color as the glass bottles in which Mrs. Riley always kept my favorite salves and perfumes. Felton, however, had a slight tint of blue in his gaze, more akin to the sea in the south at the height of summer, where the depths held untold creatures and dangers.

"Welcome to my home, Miss Shipman...and Miss...?" Felton asked.

"Miss Moon," I answered for Elizabeth. "She is my cousin."

He smiled, and it sent chills up and down my arms at how *much* he resembled Miles. "We are pleased to have you. My dear Miss Colette has spent the better part of the last twenty-four hours telling me all that she could about you."

"Has she now?" I asked, trying to maintain a relatively warm yet distant smile. I need not let anyone see my true level of excitement. "Well, I certainly enjoyed meeting her as well, of course."

Miss Colette beamed at me.

"She tells me that your father works at the stock exchange," Felton asked. "That is quite impressive."

That is not at all what I told her, but –

"Oh, he most certainly does," Elizabeth said. "He is vital to operations there. Poor girl, she hardly has seen him since the crash back in October."

"I can appreciate that," Felton said. "These are busy times."

Miss Colette hung on my arm, fluttering her eyelashes at Felton. "I already told her that *my* father works in banking, so she and I have a great deal in common, don't we?"

Felton straightened his necktie. "You certainly do. Now, shall I show you to the parlor where our other guests are waiting and enjoying some refreshments?"

"Certainly," I said, doing my best not to seem overly eager to separate myself from Miss Colette's grip.

He started down the rightmost hallway, a rounded corridor that led through the stone manor. The sound of jovial conversation drifted through the handsomely decorated space boasting exquisite portraits and carved statuettes. I saw long, polished tables of mahogany and walnut, vases filled with winter greens, exotic ornaments from far off places, and a jade elephant no larger than my hand safely enclosed behind a glass case.

"I take it the both of you are American?" Felton asked as we walked.

"Yes," I said. "Though my dear cousin has a fiancé here in London. Which reminds me...you would not mind terribly if she were to borrow your telephone so that she may contact him periodically? She does pine over him when they are apart."

Felton smirked as he regarded us. "I see no reason not to allow that. I shall have Mr. Henry show you where you may make a call in private."

"Thank you," Elizabeth said, giving him her brightest smile.

We stopped outside an open doorway, beyond which lay a parlor that would have put some of the finest I had ever seen to shame. I had never thought my family's home was poorly fashioned, as Mother only ever desired the latest and most fashionable furnishings that she could get her hands on. Even our home along the Hudson River to the north of the city, much more spacious than our house in the city, paled in comparison to Felton's house. It was difficult to imagine anyone truly living in this elegant place.

"Please, make yourselves comfortable," Felton said. "Miss Colette and I shall go and greet our remaining guests. Once everyone is here, we shall have tea in the drawing room overlooking the back gardens."

"That sounds lovely," I said. "Thank you, Mr. Beechwood."

He smiled at me before Miss Colette dragged him from the room.

Elizabeth sidled up to me, her eyes passing over the room. "All we have heard was correct. This is quite the exclusive event."

"Do you recognize some of the guests?" I asked, guiding her into the room a little further, out of the way of the door.

"I certainly do," she said. "Over in the corner near the fireplace is Sir Livingston, who was knighted after saving an entire schoolhouse of children that had caught fire. He is a sort of hero around these parts. Near the window are Mr. and Mrs. Rose, who happen to own a great many of the rowhouses north of Hyde

Park, as both of their families are extensive and numerous. They are quite prominent. Lastly, the trio sitting at the sofa and the armchairs beside it are Miss Carter, Mr. Browne, and Mr. Langley, who might seem like less impressive persons but who are in social demand these days. They are a popular newspaper columnist, a constable, and a well known attorney, respectively. Mr. Browne has been in the papers recently for resolving some criminal matter or other that has brought him a degree of fame."

"Interesting that Mr. Beechwood would feel confident enough having that lot in his home," I said.

"Or perhaps that is the precise reason why he invites those sorts," Elizabeth murmured as we continued to move around the outside of the room, stopping eventually at the grand piano tucked away in the further corner. "He wants to continually provide the illusion that he has nothing to hide."

"A good thought," I said.

Elizabeth smirked. "Interesting that Miss Colette seems to have taken such an interest in you."

"Rather unfortunate now that we're here, I'm afraid," I said. "I should much rather pass this trip without any notice at all."

"She is fascinated with you," Elizabeth said. "I wonder why."

"I believe she thinks that I am a worthy connection," I said. "Or that I have useful connections in New

York. Then again, she might merely be desperate for entertainment and new faces."

"True," Elizabeth said. "And did you know what else I noticed?"

"What?" I asked.

Her eyes narrowed as she also turned away from the rest of those in the room to ensure they would not overhear us. "He looks a great deal like your butler."

My heart skipped. "I thought the very same. Which explains how he was able to get away with – well, with you know – in the first place. If the two look so much alike, of course he could pass as Miles."

"Indeed," Elizabeth said. "It is quite striking, really, the resemblance between them."

"They could almost be brothers…" I said.

She nodded. "Well, now what?" she asked. "Do we play along? Or shall we try and sneak off as soon as we can?"

"No, I do not think we should go anywhere right now," I said. "We have all weekend, although the sooner we can find what we need, the sooner we can leave. If we do not get our chance today, perhaps tomorrow we can use one of your calls with – what should we call him?"

"Peter is fine," Elizabeth said. "They won't know who he is. Anyway, that sounds like a good idea. That should give us the out we need, and without looking suspicious."

"That is my hope as well," I said.

"What should we be looking for?" she asked.

"Beechwood will not betray himself when his guests are around," I said. "So it will not be in anything he says. Nor do I believe he will have left anything out in the open that could incriminate him."

"True," Elizabeth said.

"The best we can do right now is to remain in the background," I said. "Go unnoticed. Not try terribly hard to get to know anyone here. We shall have to pretend to be aloof, or disinterested, or even act as if we believe ourselves to be their betters. I do not particularly care, as long as we don't draw any unnecessary attention to ourselves."

"Precisely," Elizabeth said. "We need only keep our heads bent together, and no one should dare disturb us."

"Of course," I said. I drew in a deep breath, my heart still fluttering uncomfortably in my chest. "Soon enough, we will find an opening where we might be able to sneak off and go look for something in his personal quarters. We will have to be certain that no one will notice us, and that he will be otherwise occupied. The time will come. We must simply be ready for it."

"Right, right," Elizabeth said. She shuddered, but her determined expression persisted. "You were right when you said this would feel a great deal different when we were here."

I glanced sidelong at her. "Are you having second thoughts?"

"No," she said. "I am here to help you. Fear will not diminish my resolve."

"Because if you believe we must, we can call Peter and – "

"No," she said, more insistent this time. "I will remain here. You need not worry, nor should you have to take this on all alone."

"Well, thank you again," I said. "It will be much easier to tackle if we do it together."

"That is my hope, as well," she said. She grinned at me. "What are friends for, if not to help investigate a murder?"

It was not long before Felton Beechwood and Miss Colette returned to bring us all to the drawing room for tea. The tea was impressive, with a wide spread of selections ranging from imported teas from Japan and China, as well as a few from India. My favorite happened to be an Earl Grey from Yorkshire, along with a honey that had apparently come from an apiary in France.

Elizabeth and I chatted quietly between ourselves until, only a short while later, we were taken off again, this time to the dining room for dinner.

The dining room smelled of roasted lamb and fennel, and I had not realized how hungry I was.

We took our seats at the table, and to my great dislike, they had arranged for us to sit across the table from the parties we had come with. Elizabeth gave me a worried look as she took her seat, acknowledging what I had known, that we would not be able to talk about anything more during the duration of the meal.

Well, I suppose we could always speak later when we have the chance to reconvene. Perhaps before we tuck in to bed for the evening, I thought.

Drinks were served as Felton sat down at the head of the table, Miss Colette directly to his left. He smiled around at all of his guests.

"I cannot tell you how grateful I am that all of you have come this weekend," Felton said, holding his glass aloft. "We may well enjoy these retreats once every few weeks, but it is always so wonderfully refreshing when I have both old, familiar faces, as well as those whom I hope to call new friends. I hope that you all find benefit in this as much as Colette and I do, with the chance to meet new people and have new acquaintances."

"Here, here, Mr. Beechwood," said the man Elizabeth had indicated as Sir Livingston. He also raised his glass, cheering his host.

"Many of you have been introduced, but some of you may not know our newest friends, Miss Shipman and her cousin, Miss Moon," Miss Colette said. She grinned, ear to ear. "I imagine a great many of you will be interested to know that Miss Shipman's father is one of the financial gurus of New York's Wall Street, a man of vital importance at the stock exchange."

My word, this story grows more absurd with each telling, I thought. "Oh, Miss Colette, you are too – " I said, but noticed the flash in Elizabeth's eyes, warning me not to correct her. And she was right, of course. This could only work in my favor. *This* Miss Shipman that I was portraying did not truly exist. What did it matter to any of these people if she was real or not? I would never be seeing any of them again anyway. "You are far too kind," I finished.

Miss Colette twittered with laughter. "Modest, isn't she? And clever. She told me over tea last night that she not only spent a great deal of time at the galleries in New York, but also at the race tracks." She grinned at Felton, her expression melting with adoration. "You would certainly know a thing or two about that, would you not?"

Mr. Beechwood watched me closely, a small smile playing at the corner of his mouth. "I may well," he said. "Tell me, Miss Shipman, as cultured as you are, surely you find our city worth the time to explore?"

There was one thing to be said of Londoners, and that was their evident pride in their city. People in New York felt much the same, but a bit rougher around the edges. Many of us would never admit to loving our city, instead finding reasons to complain. I heard Joan speak this way quite regularly, especially with friends from out of town.

I decided it was best to adopt the same sort of disdain. I did not need this conversation to dwell on me and this pretend life I had made up any longer.

"Oh, London is a breath of fresh air," I said. "A bit small, despite its age, I suppose. New York has a great many of the same amenities...but I must admit that I have grown bored of them. It has been a welcome change to see something new for a time."

"I am pleased to hear it," Mr. Beechwood said.

There, that should suffice, I thought, reaching for my own drink. Now the conversation could move naturally on without keeping the attention on me.

"Miss Shipman, you said your father works at the stock exchange?" asked Mr. Langley, the attorney. He leaned around Miss Carter to eye me, his right eye as round as that of a fish behind his silver monocle. "I have a cousin who works there. One of the advisors, you see. Perhaps you know a Mr. Tillman?"

"No, sir, I cannot say that I do," I said with a dismissive, disinterested wave. I did not want this attention, did not want to continue this conversation. "My apologies."

"How is New York these days?" asked Sir

Livingston. "I have not been in almost ten years. I imagine it is still growing, changing as it ever does?"

"I suppose I hardly notice the change if it comes," I said.

"Perhaps you are so accustomed to change that you take no notice," Felton Beechwood said with a chuckle. "Not that I am terribly surprised. One always hears stories of New York, and the impact it leaves on people."

"Darling, you *must* tell her about your recent time there," Miss Colette said before her head swiveled around to look at me. "It is a wonder that the pair of you did not cross paths before today. He would surely have met some of your father's acquaintances, as he would only have met with those of the wealthiest class in New York."

"Yes, it is rather strange that we did not cross paths," I said. "Well, the city is a big place. I suspect you were not there quite long enough to have been introduced to my father's friends." That was partially true, of course, but given what I knew now, it was probably the other way around; I may not have graced the same upper circles that he might have been parading around in.

"Perhaps not," he said, but he still seemed amused.

I have seen Miles wear that face when he is thinking something that he does not want to let on, I realized.

"I must admit, I have always had an interest in New

York, as I've never been," said Miss Carter. "Are the buildings truly as large as they say? They may as well touch the sky?"

"Hardly," I said with a laugh. "You will have to forgive me, but I have lived there all my life, and it may not awe me as much as it might visitors. It is the largest city that I have ever seen, and by far the most impressive...but the stories I hear of it do make me laugh."

Miss Carter's face fell, and she tried to give me a smile. "I see," she said.

"Oh, but do not let that deter you from visiting," I said, crossing my arms smoothly, tilting my chin up ever so slightly. I despised these sorts of women, yet here I was portraying one. I supposed I had watched enough of them to know how to carry myself. "Please, come and experience the world's best and finest in every field. Truly, you will be stunned. I suppose I have a lack of want, and am spoiled." I chortled, and Elizabeth joined in with me as if we shared a private joke.

"She is not wrong, you know," Felton said, spinning his glass by the stem clutched between his thumb and forefinger. "Often the stories of the city are blown a great deal out of proportion. It has its drawbacks, much like every other city on the rest of the globe."

I glanced down the table at him, surprised by his thoughtful comment.

I had come to his home expecting a murderous lout, but the man who sat at the end of the table was as refined as his cousin, well spoken, kind, and attentive to the thoughts of others. He was even agreeable, from what I had seen thus far.

It infuriated me. I knew that, in different circumstances, I would be inclined to like him, given his similarity to Miles, but that only made it all the more difficult. The worst part was that he was not being intentionally charming. He had no idea who I was, or why I was really there. He truly thought me to be nothing more than a guest at his home for a party. It was quite troubling.

I would have to keep my guard up all the more, lest I allowed my affection for Miles to cloud my judgment of the man who had killed his wife.

Dinner carried on without further incident. Just as I had hoped, the conversation slipped away past me like a leaf being carried along a lazy stream. The guests spoke of other events and affairs happening in London, and while I listened carefully and watched Felton for any sign or hint, none appeared. The distance between his murder of Sophia and the current time was too great for it to be brought up in ordinary conversation, and I imagined that some of the guests present would have been wise enough not to bring it up to him in the first place.

The party adjourned back to the parlor after dinner that evening for games and some music. Elizabeth lingered near the chess set with me, as it was a game which we knew we could not be bothered while playing, her eyes darting over toward the grand piano in the corner.

Miss Colette had taken a seat there, her fingers trilling the keys with a practiced lightness that impressed everyone in the room. She picked up a tune from a musical that I had heard once before, and began belting out the melody at the top of her lungs with a profound and surprising accuracy that had me stunned to silence for a moment or two.

"Well, she must have attracted him somehow," Elizabeth murmured, nodding her head in Felton's direction. "Look at the way he is watching her now."

It was true. He seemed as enraptured as the rest of the guests, staying by her side at the piano as she played for us.

"Though, that is not the same way that...well, you know who watches you," she went on. "Mr. Beechwood seems to care for her, but I do not believe his affection to be terribly deep."

"Why not?" I asked. It surprised me she had been paying that close attention to their relationship, when all I had wanted to do was watch him. *I should be wiser than that. It would do me well to watch her too, wouldn't it?* I reprimanded myself.

"I just have the sense that her attachment is stronger than his," she said with a shrug. "That is my hunch. It also has surprised me a great deal that he seems...normal. I half expected a raving lunatic when we came here."

"He is not what I expected, either," I said. "Miles said that some people have called his cousin's behavior paranoid, and that he had become suspicious of everyone around him."

"I would say he is certainly cautious," Elizabeth said. "But not to an extreme, as he is inviting perfect strangers into his home on a regular basis."

"True..." I said.

Elizabeth looked sidelong at me, her eyes bright. "Are you quite sure that this is the man we are looking for?" she whispered. "Is it possible Miles was wrong?"

An unsettling feeling crept down my spine, as she gave voice to the same thought that had occurred to me as well.

"He just doesn't seem the dangerous type," she went on.

I did not respond immediately.

"...Sylvia?"

"I know," I said. "I don't think Miles is wrong...but it does make me wonder if this whole affair is not quite as clear as he might have thought."

12

Elizabeth and I lay awake for quite some time that night, debating whether or not we should take advantage of the dark. My thought had been to explore, using the excuse of looking for the washroom if we were caught. Elizabeth agreed, unable to sleep, and so we set off just before midnight.

We were not caught, but we also learned that these weekend retreats were not meant for a great deal of sleeping. Elizabeth and I overheard a conversation between some of the men who had taken to the study to smoke cigars after the rest of the women had gone to bed for the evening. They spoke of nothing in particular, recent race winnings and the price of swine. We wandered through the halls, trying to make sense of the place, but when we heard the footsteps of the men retiring for the night, we hurried back to our room and shut ourselves in to wait for morning.

I had not expected to find something the moment I started looking, but I had hoped that we might find a direction to follow.

"The trouble is that the house is enormous," Elizabeth said the following morning. "We might well take an entire week to scour it from top to bottom."

I frowned, staring down into my teacup. "You are right," I said, keeping my voice low. "It all seems so..."

"Formal?" Elizabeth finished for me. "It does not feel truly lived in. Hardly any personal touches."

"Which means that we have not found the places we need to look through yet," I said. "From what Miles has told me, this is his cousin's permanent residence, and likely where he would keep such things."

I looked around the library that Elizabeth and I had been shown to this morning, a quiet place where we could relax and talk before breakfast. Mr. Henry had brought some tea to warm us as we waited for the rest of the guests to rouse for the day.

"It is quite astounding that none of the guests are awake yet," Elizabeth said, drawing her tea to her face, allowing the steam to brush against her cheeks. "These sorts of folks I suppose have little responsibility to get them up early in the morning."

"And as late as many of them stayed awake last

night..." I said. "Well, no matter. It's given us a chance to plan and have a think."

"True," she said, gazing around the library. A large window behind us allowed some of the bright morning sun inside, though the shelves had been placed strategically around so as not to be washed in the light, protecting the spines from damage. "I wonder if we might find a clue in here."

"Apart from what Mr. Beechwood prefers in literature, I doubt it," I said. "I suppose we could take each book off the shelves and page through them looking for hidden notes or some such, but I have no reason to believe that is how he might have chosen to hide his guilt."

"Suddenly three days doesn't seem like nearly enough time to look around," Elizabeth said.

"Our best chance at this point is to find an opportunity to search for Beechwood's personal study," I said.

"What would you say to looking now?" Elizabeth asked. "As it is just – "

Her words trailed off as voices echoed down the hall, closely followed by a raucous laugh. She looked at me, eyebrows raised.

*Too bad for us, we should have taken the chance a half hour ago...*I thought.

Miss Carter, Mr. Langley, and Sir Livingston came wandering into the library, Mr. Langley stretching his arms high over his head.

"Good morning," Miss Carter said to us with a subtle wave, looking as stunning as she had the night before. The trio made their way past us to another table near the window, and Mr. Henry appeared as if out of the wall itself to offer them tea just as he had for us.

Elizabeth glanced toward the door. "Shall we...take a walk before breakfast?" she asked.

"I should like that," I said. We could easily use the excuse that we were just stretching our legs before breakfast. As there were other guests getting up and finally joining the rest of the household, we could be seen as doing the same.

We left our tea and started back down the hall. The estate, quiet and still in the frosted morning, would have certainly been a pleasant place to meander through if we were not so determined to find evidence against Felton Beechwood.

"Where should we begin?" Elizabeth asked in a low voice, lacing her hand through the crook in my arm.

"I should think upstairs, if we can make it," I said. "I cannot imagine that he would keep anything terribly personal on the lower floors that could be discovered by some of his guests on these weekends."

"True," Elizabeth said. "Very good, then. I shall be glad to have you here, though, for my sense of direction is terrible, and I am perfectly sure that I will get lost."

"It should not be terribly difficult," I said. "As long as we keep in mind that we aren't to wander into places that we may not be allowed in."

"But I thought that was precisely where we were trying to go," Elizabeth said, dropping her voice all the further.

I smirked at her. "Yes, but no one can know we are *meaning* to go to those places. For now, the house is still so new to us that I believe we shall be able to get away with it."

"I see," she said, returning the smirk. "Then let us see what we can – "

A silhouette at the end of the hall caused her to clamp her mouth shut and draw even nearer to me.

I understood why, because if I had not had my wits about me, I might well have thought it to be Miles coming toward us. Tired as I was, the worry permeated through my whole being, making me cautious enough not to blurt out his name.

Felton Beechwood stepped into a pool of light as he passed by one of the windows lining the outer hall. He was wearing an easy smile, his hair damp at the ends. "Good morning, ladies," he said. "I am pleased to see that I am not the only person keen to get an early start."

"You are certainly not alone," I said, hoping he could not hear the thunderous roar of my heartbeat pounding inside my chest. "Though I can hardly blame your other guests, given the fun that we all enjoyed late last night."

A smile stretched across his face. "I hope you ladies enjoyed yourselves as well?"

"Oh, yes," I said.

"I noticed you playing chess," he said. "And I saw that Miss Moon has quite the eye for the game."

Elizabeth blushed, her gaze darting away.

"My cousin has always had a sharp eye," I said. "Though we do apologize for being rather invested in our own game. She is a bit shy, you see."

"I have wondered if that was the case," Felton said, his smile still warm. "No matter. The whole point of these weekends is to enjoy one's self away from the busyness of the city, you see. I should not like for anyone to feel awkward or out of sorts while they are here."

*Interesting that he shouldn't want anyone out of sorts...*I thought.

"Well, there is still some time before breakfast," he said. "And Miss Colette has taken to trying on every dress that she brought with her this weekend. Would either of you care for a small tour around the estate?"

I perked up. What a perfect excuse to be able to explore without the fear of being caught. "Oh, Mr. Beechwood, would you?" I asked. "I do so love these old homes in the countryside, and would be ever so grateful to have a glimpse of some of this one's secrets."

I noticed a new glow in his gaze, almost mischievous. "I knew that you and I would get on well. We are cut from the same cloth, wanting to see only the interesting bits."

I tossed my hair, sighing. "You must forgive me, Mr. Beechwood, but I come from the land of the interesting and unique. You will have to understand precisely why I desire to see such things."

"Always chasing the next excitement," he said. "Very well, I certainly hope that I will be able to satisfy your curiosity."

"I suppose we shall have to wait and see," I said, smirking up at him.

When I imagined I was speaking with Miles, it became a great deal easier to speak with Felton. Some of the nerves abated, and I knew *how* to talk with him. He seemed to take the playful chiding as well as Miles did, and even responded to it in a similar manner.

"Allow me to show you some of my favorite spots," he said. "As I have spent a great majority of my life in this place, I know practically everything there is to know about it."

"Do tell, then," I said. "Enthrall us with your knowledge."

He offered his arm to me, which I only hesitated to take for a brief moment by glancing at Elizabeth. "Never fear, I shall walk with her, as well. I see that the pair of you will not be separated."

"We certainly shall not be," I said. "My cousin is very dear to me, you see, and I will not allow her fears to get the better of her."

"Well, I shall not either," Mr. Beechwood said. "Please be at ease, Miss Moon. My only desire is that my guests enjoy themselves to the utmost." He extended his arm to her, and she smiled at him as she took it.

We started down the hall, and I expected to feel somewhat uneasy about walking arm in arm with a murderer...but instead, I only felt numb. I thought back to the times where I had been in the presence of a murderer, only to discover the truth later. *At least now I know the truth,* I thought. *And can respond as I should. This is not at all like the situation with Mr. Opal in Rhode Island. I will not have to reprimand myself for being around him when I would have surely acted differently had I known, not allowed myself to like him —*

There was no danger of that here. Felton may very well look like Miles, act like him, even share the same blood...but he was not the man that I had come to trust wholeheartedly with my life. He could never measure up, nor would he ever be able to say or do anything so charming that it would change my mind about what Miles had said he had done. All I needed to do was continue this illusion so that he would continue to fall for it...and then get out of here before he ever learned the truth.

I knew it was inevitable that he would find out what I had done, but I hoped that it would be as the police were taking him away in handcuffs, ready to try him for a murder long since unsolved.

This thought stirred me on, straightening my back and drawing a smile to my face. Once this was over, Miles could be who he should be and end all the secrecy.

"This house is over one hundred years old," Mr. Beechwood said, turning slowly with Elizabeth and I down yet another window-lined hall, streaming with sunlight. "Built by my great great uncle, Nicholas Beechwood the first."

Nicholas? I thought. Isn't that what Mr. Daniels had referred to Miles as when we met with him some weeks ago? The day that he told me I could trust Miles? I hoped the surprise was not visible on my face.

"My ancestor fashioned it after the style of a castle that he had loved as a child in Scotland. Lacking the same type of stone that had been used in his ideal, he managed to locate a lake a short distance away that he pulled rock from. This stone seems to have suited his taste, and as you can see, the house still stands."

"It is a beautiful piece of architecture," I said. "One of the best I have seen during my time here in London."

"Thank you," he said. "It pales in comparison to the home that my uncle lives in near Gloucestershire. That is a real castle." He frowned. "Though I have not spoken with that side of my family in some time, as they have endured a rather tremendous tragedy."

"Oh...how unfortunate for them," I said.

"Indeed," he said, but his smile returned as we stopped outside a door. "Now, this room is particularly special, as it has a solitary use." He reached out and pushed the door open.

A rush of air brushed against my senses, bringing the scent of damp earth and plant matter out into the hall. I peered inside the dark space, and found a room entirely lined with wood, filled with every manner of sprouts that I could think of. Each had a small label, all being prepared for spring planting.

"Mr. Henry has quite the talent for plants, and as such, he brings them all in here to prepare and water and feed," Felton said.

"What of the sunlight?" Elizabeth asked.

"Oh, that's quite simple," Felton said, striding across the small space. He reached out and pulled at an imperceptible space on the wall, and a shutter gave way to a large, circular window. Brilliant light washed into the room, bathing the potted infant leaves. "I am certain he will not mind if they have some more light today. He always comes in to water them at the top of the nine o'clock hour."

"What a charming space," I said, and I hated the fact that it gave me ideas for our own sprouting back in New York. *Joan would love a room like this...*I thought.

"On to the next treasure," he said. "Do not worry, I realize full well that it might not have been terribly interesting, but it is an important part of our estate none the less."

"I found it quite interesting," Elizabeth said. "What else can you tell us of your home?"

He led us up a narrow set of stairs at the end of the hall, letting out into a study on the second floor, hidden behind a bookshelf.

I hid a frown. *If these are the sorts of passages within this house, then how can I possibly find what I am looking for?* I wondered. I reprimanded myself as he closed the shelf behind us, smiling proudly at us. *No, focus, Sylvia. It will only work for your benefit that he is showing you where all these secrets are.*

"This is a study only accessed by that little staircase," he said. "When my grandfather lived here, he cut the room off from the hall, sealed it in, and had the bookcase door made. He wanted to make sure that he could have complete privacy when he was in here. I took it for myself when I was young."

I looked around, my eyes falling on each and every corner of the room. "So this is your personal study?" I asked. "It is impressive."

"No, actually, it isn't," he said. "My personal study is up on the top floor of the house, and only a few people have laid eyes on it." He smirked. "My apologies, ladies, but as it is a place where most of my business is conducted, I am not able to show it to you."

My heart sank, but I fixed a smile on my face.

"What a charming picture," Elizabeth said, wandering over to one of the shelves along the far wall. She gazed at one of the photographs in a small frame tucked in on one of the shelves. "I did not realize that you had a twin, Mr. Beechwood."

I glanced at the picture, and my stomach twisted into knots. That wasn't his twin, that was –

I looked over at Felton Beechwood, and a darkness passed over his face for a brief moment, before fading behind his smile as he chuckled. He approached the framed photograph, picking it up off the shelf. "How interesting that you would think he and I look alike. No, that is my cousin. Unfortunately...he is dead."

He walked over to the desk, pulled open a drawer, and slipped the picture inside.

Elizabeth gave me a look with raised brows before turning away to survey the room once again.

I had to try again. This tour, as interesting as it was, did not seem to be leading me any closer to what I needed to find. "Mr. Beechwood..." I said, knowing full well that I was testing my boundaries. "Where do you often spend your time, then? Do you have a favorite room in which to while away the hours? I can imagine that the places that do not often have guests may be more comfortable."

He smiled at me, and it sent shivers down my spine as it felt as if Miles was peering down at me with the same sort of grin. "Oh, Miss Shipman, I am sorry to say that it would not be at all interesting to you," he said. "I am a humble man with humble enjoyments. I have done a great deal to ensure that the occupied parts of the estate are fun and engaging, but have not spent much effort on improving my own quarters." He tilted his head. "Perhaps I shall have to look into that, for the time when I finally settle down and marry."

My face flushed at the way he looked at me. "Oh, I am certain Miss Colette will appreciate that."

He chuckled, walking back toward the bookcase. "I suppose she would, wouldn't she?" he murmured.

We started back down the staircase when Felton looked over at me, a perplexed expression on his face. "You know...you remind me of someone I once knew..." he said.

I didn't know what to make of that.

"Do I? Well, I certainly hope she was someone pleasant," I said.

He smiled, but said nothing more.

We reached the end of the hall, Felton telling us about the billiard room that he had planned a bit of a tournament for that evening in, when Miss Colette appeared around the corner.

At first, her face blossomed into a bright smile, but when her gaze fell upon me, still arm in arm with Felton, a different look darkened her gorgeous features.

"Darling," she said, hurrying over to him and throwing herself into his arms. Her weight managed to disentangle his arm from mine, forcing him to grab hold of her so that she did not slip down to the floor. "Oh, I *wondered* where you had gotten off to this morning," she crooned. She shot me another sharp look, snaking her arm through his, steering him down the hall.

"My apologies, Colette, I was just showing some of our guests around, helping them feel welcome," Felton said as they made their way around the corner.

"Yes, well, there are more important matters for you to attend to," Miss Colette said. "Namely me, of course, as well as breakfast. Come along, now, dear." She tittered with laughter, high and shrill.

Elizabeth glanced at me, shaking her head. "Well?" she asked. "What do you suggest we do now?"

"I suppose we shall have to continue to bide our time," I said, my heart sinking. "If only he had been willing to show us his personal study."

"I imagine he wouldn't want to because that is precisely where we need to go," she said.

"That was my thought, too," I said. "All right. Then we need to find an opening to slip away and go look for that room. It will take some time, being high up in the house as he said it was."

"And we will be expected for breakfast now," Elizabeth said. "People will be suspicious if we do not join them."

"Especially Mr. Beechwood," I said. I sighed. "All right. Let us join them. Maybe we will hear something else useful."

13

We had no opportunity to sneak off for the next several hours. After breakfast, we were given a tour of the stables out back, and then we were whisked off to the pond at the back of the estate where we walked out on the dock and enjoyed some of the warm, spring air.

I caught Mr. Beechwood stealing glances of me every once in a while, and he did little to hide them. He smiled when he realized I was watching him, too, before returning to speaking with the other guests.

As we were making our way back up to the manor, the sun broke through the clouds, which caused everyone to pause and gaze up at it. It was a beautiful sight, seeing the extensive property bathed in the warm, golden light.

"Well, I'll be..." Mr. Langley said, planting his

hands on his hips. "I cannot remember the last time I have seen the sun. Perhaps November?"

"We should take full advantage of it," said Sir Livingston.

"Right you are," said Mr. Langley. He looked around at all the gentlemen present. "What say you all to a rousing game of cricket?"

"What a splendid idea!" exclaimed Miss Colette. "It will give us all a chance to cheer you on, and tire you all out before dinner this evening!"

Elizabeth glanced at me, and I sighed. Our time at the estate was growing short. This was our only full day on the property, and we would be leaving by midday tomorrow. I needed to find some clues or this entire trip would be a waste.

The gentlemen quickly prepared a game, all of the equipment acquired from a shed near the stables, and several servants drafted to even out the numbers. They did not even give us ladies a chance to go inside to change or ready ourselves, as they were far too eager to begin the game.

Mr. Henry and some of the other servants brought seats for us ladies to sit upon, along with some parasols for the sun.

Elizabeth and I chose a pair of chairs off to the side, partially tucked beneath the shade of a beech tree. I gazed up at it, feeling a slight chill at the sight of the family namesake of both Miles and Felton.

Elizabeth settled in beside me, sipping the lemonade that had been brought out to all of us. "What are you thinking?" she asked around the lip of her glass before taking a small sip.

"I am frustrated," I said in a low voice, watching as the men set up the first round of the game. All the guests were out of earshot, but I did not want to take the chance of the wind carrying our words further than we would want. "We have hardly had the chance to explore the manor, nor the opportunity to sneak away to do so. If we parted from the group during any of these outdoor activities, our absence would be noticed."

"I have thought the same," she said, swirling the lemon slices around in her glass. "I suppose the best chance we shall have is after everyone goes to sleep this evening."

I frowned. "And that will hardly be enough time. Only one chance, and what if we come up empty-handed?"

Elizabeth said nothing, her eyes drifting over toward the others. She straightened, a stricken expression passing over her face.

"What's the matter?" I asked.

"Miss Colette..." she said. "She's coming this way and she does not look terribly pleased."

*Oh no...*I thought. There was no way she could have learned the truth, was there?

She wore a cold smile, her eyes fixed squarely upon me as she drew closer.

I did my best to smile at her, giving her a little wave. It was best to feign ignorance...which was rather easy to do, considering that I had no earthly idea why she was suddenly chilly toward me.

"It seems that this is the perfect chance for us to have a little chat..." she said, her tone acidic. Her mouth twisted into a frown, as she brushed some of her dark hair from her face as the wind caught it. "Tell me, do you think you are funny, Miss Shipman?"

I blinked up at her. "Well, no, not particularly," I said. "Though I certainly thought that you and I had been getting on well enough – "

"*That* was before you started to flutter your eyelashes at Felton," she hissed, her hands balling into fists at her side. "How *dare* you try to steal him and his attention away from me?"

I gaped at her. "Miss Colette, I assure you, I am doing no such thing – "

"Do not lie to me," she said, her eyes narrowing to slits. "I caught you wandering around with him this morning before breakfast. I saw the way the pair of you were gazing at one another."

"You are greatly mistaken," I said quickly. "I have no interest in your Mr. Beechwood, not in the least – "

"Felton is a simple man with simple desires," she said. "He wants a quiet life, and while I have done my best to ensure he has that, when he sees someone like *you*, it seems to have addled his mind for some reason, making him think that he wants something – or someone – else entirely!"

I could hardly keep up with her train of thought.

She took the opportunity to step closer, gazing down at me with great dislike. "You cannot fool me. You were trying to catch his eye, and have been since the moment you set foot in the manor. I should never have asked you to come here, never should have – "

"Miss Colette, I truly believe you misunderstand," I said. "Mr. Beechwood told me quite plainly that I simply remind him of someone that he once knew."

"Oh?" she prodded. "Then pray tell me who that person is."

I hesitated. "He did not say, but I assume that may be why he has been treating me as you have said," I said.

She crossed her arms over her body, turning away. "I never should have invited you," she hissed. "You would do well to *stay away* from him. He has no interest in anyone apart from *me*, so you may as well stop trying – "

"Truly, you must hear me when I say that I am not at all interested," I said. "If you would have given me the chance to speak, you would know that I am also engaged. I am to be married in June."

I didn't know where that particular lie came from, but I was desperate to calm her down.

She gave an annoyed wave, as if swatting at a fly. "I do not want to hear what you have to say," she said. Then she lowered herself down so that she and I stared at one another, eye to eye. "You will go about the rest of this retreat without saying another word to him, unless I am around. If you do not keep your distance..." She dropped her voice even further. "Then you will have to answer to *me*...and I can assure you that you shall be displeased if you do."

With that, she straightened up and strode off, her hips swaying ever so slightly as if in victory.

I stared after her, stunned into silence.

"I had thought she rather liked you," Elizabeth said after a few moments, breaking the uncomfortable silence between us. The cricket game continued on, none of the guests or the players any wiser about our little confrontation with Miss Colette.

"As did I..." I said, dismayed. "How have I drawn so much attention to myself? When all I wanted was to do anything but?"

"Cheer up, Sylvie," Elizabeth murmured, her eyes following after Miss Colette, who had gracefully eased herself back down into her own lawn chair, pretending as if the two of us did not exist. "It isn't all that bad. Now that we're here, you don't especially need her friendship any longer."

"Maybe I don't," I said, the knots in my chest snaking around one another as if attempting to weave some sort of anxious basket. "But I now have both her and Mr. Beechwood watching me, which is going to make it all the more impossible to go and look for his private study."

"Oh..." Elizabeth said. "I suppose you're right. If he is interested in you, as he seems to be – "

"He is not interested," I said, not bothering to keep the frustration from my voice. "Miss Colette was simply seeing what her own insecurities made her believe to be there."

Elizabeth lifted an eyebrow. "I am not so sure about that," she said. Then she shrugged. "But now you have his eye, as well as hers watching to make sure the both of you do not pair off again."

"Right," I said, my head falling back against the lawn chair. I gazed up at the sky as blue as a robin's egg, with wispy clouds lazily trailing across with no particular place to go.

"Well, then the answer is simple, isn't it?" Elizabeth asked. "We simply need to come up with some sort of distraction."

I raised my head, eyeing her. "That's not a bad idea," I said, the first spark of hope flaring in my chest like sunlight peeking through a curtain into a dark room. "Did you have something in mind?"

Elizabeth smirked, leaning closer to me. "As a

matter of fact, I do," she said, her smile growing. "I could fake something, an injury or some such, which would give you the time that you would need."

"You're not serious," I said, glaring at her. "Elizabeth, that is foolishness – "

"Let me finish," she said. "I will not truly harm myself, but it will have to be believable, and something that could allow you to slip away for a lengthy period of time."

"You don't think anyone would notice my absence if you were hurt?" I asked.

"I imagine their attention would be on me," she said. "At least, that would be my hope."

I shook my head. "No, absolutely not. You would be in danger, being around Mr. Beechwood without me, and I promised your fiancé that I would watch out for you."

"No, I would not be in any danger," she said. "I would be with a crowd of people. He would not dare to do anything to me, or anyone else for that matter, in front of everyone. I would be perfectly safe. *You* would be the one in danger, sneaking around as you would be."

I licked my lips. "This is insanity, you know that?"

She grinned. "But you do not hate the idea, do you?"

It was difficult to argue with her about that. If we could not *find* the chance to slip away, maybe she was right that we would have to *make* the chance. "I still don't like it," I said.

"Of course you don't," she said. "But you know as well as I that this could be our only chance."

I hesitated for a long moment, watching the cricket game absently. Mr. Langley made an excellent pass to Felton, who quickly turned around and scored a point on Sir Livingston who was playing for the opposite side. The men cheered, hurrying to one another to shake hands.

"What did you have in mind, then?" I asked.

She beamed at me.

14

The afternoon brought rain, the clouds swelling and choosing to dump their contents upon the cricket players, all of whom had pink cheeks, foreheads, and ears kissed by the sun. They hurried inside, helping us ladies to get out of the wet as quickly as possible. Mr. Langley laughed, Mr. Browne commenting about how it might have been for the best, for he and Sir Livingston would have surely come back to win the game had they been given just a few more plays.

"Some towels to dry off, sir," Mr. Henry said, coming up to us with a stack in his arms. He passed them out to us all, allowing us the chance to pad our faces dry.

"Feel free to excuse yourself to change, ladies, if you feel so led," Felton said with a grin. "I should not like to ask any young ladies to remain in sodden clothing and catch their deaths."

Miss Colette chortled, shrill in the echoing hall. "Shall we reconvene in the drawing room in fifteen minutes?" she asked. "And I should absolutely love to read a play all together once again."

"That sounds a wonderful way to pass the time until dinner," Felton said. "We shall see you all then. I will go and find a play we can act out."

"No, I already have one in mind," Miss Colette said, threading her arm through his at the same moment she shot me a nasty look. "I shall accompany you. No reason for you to be alone, Felton."

The two departed, along with the other guests to their respective rooms to change.

"Shall we go and give Peter a call?" asked Elizabeth.

"That's a good idea," I said.

We headed out to the study that Felton had showed us the day before, and called up Mr. Walton. I sat in a nearby chair, trying not to openly listen, but catching snippets of the conversation. He obviously asked if we had learned anything, eagerly awaiting a yes so that he might send a driver out to fetch us, but of course I knew that Elizabeth was not able to give him the answer he hoped for. From her responses, it seemed he was not all together excited about our plan, as little as she described it, but she promised him that she would be just fine. We needed to do so in order for me to find a chance to get away. Regardless, she gave him a vague encouragement that things would work out, and that she would be seeing him tomorrow. I could tell by the look on her face that she had hoped she would have better news to share with him by now, but it was not to be for the moment.

Our fifteen minutes came to an end. Although she and I both felt we had hardly been rained upon enough to need a change, we went upstairs briefly to freshen up, before heading toward the drawing room. Elizabeth peered in through the crack between the double doors, and nodded; we would not be alone with Felton and Miss Colette.

Laughter drifted through the door as we strode inside, hardly noticed by anyone apart from Miss Colette, and unfortunately, Felton.

"Oh, come sit by me, ladies," Mr. Langley said warmly, patting the settee beside him.

"These pretty girls have no interest in sitting with someone like you," Miss Carter said with a chortle, taking a draw from her teacup. She had gone to change after our time outdoors, now sporting a pale blouse and a fitted skirt of moss green. "Leave them be. You are too persistent."

Mr. Langley gave her a childish sneer, and the two began to bicker.

I searched the room, ignoring Felton's lingering

gaze, and gestured to a chaise and armchair near the windows at the back of the room.

I watched Elizabeth closely as she took the seat in the chaise, my heart in my throat. Worry welled up within me as I realized what might well happen next.

Miss Colette cleared her throat, stepping up in front of the room with a hefty tome in her hand. "We are going to be acting out the parts of *A Rose is a Rose,*" she said. "However, there are only two female parts. I am sorry, Miss Shipman, Miss Moon, but Miss Carter and I will be playing them, if you do not mind."

"Not at all," I said. She thought she was punishing us, but in fact, she was only helping us.

"That's perfectly all right..." Elizabeth said to me, loudly enough for others to hear. "I am feeling somewhat out of sorts. Perhaps it was the sun."

My brow furrowed. "How do you mean?" I asked.

"Just a little dizzy, is all," she said with a wave. "I will be all right."

"Very well..." I said, giving her yet another wary look.

I noticed Miss Carter's gaze turning away to get to her feet as I looked at her. Had she heard?

I felt the gaze of another guest, and out of the corner of my eye I saw Mr. Langley watching us, as well, just as Miss Colette started to dramatically read through the first few lines of dialogue of her character.

For a short time, we listened to the actors, Felton Beechwood being a great deal less confident than Miss Colette, who saw no reason not to throw herself against him and bat her eyes at him, professing great love and heartache. Sir Livingston chuckled as Mr. Browne, also dragged into the performance, tripped on the leg of one of the armchairs while getting up to start the part that Miss Colette had arranged for him to play.

Elizabeth swayed beside me, grabbing hold of the arm of the chaise.

I reached out to steady her. "Elizabeth, are you quite sure you are well?" I asked.

"I'm perfectly...perfectly fine," she said, giving her head a shake.

Mr. Langley turned in his seat, his brow furrowing. "Miss Moon, would you care for some water? Or perhaps something to eat?"

Elizabeth gave another wave, smiling at him. "No, no, I am quite all right."

A few more moments passed, where Miss Colette fumbled through a difficult monologue, laughing with Miss Carter as she did so. The rest of the guests seemed enthralled with the performance, though I imagined it was because of how tremendously poor it was turning out to be.

"My darling, I shall never forget the night thou came to me with sweet songs upon thine lips," Miss

Colette cooed at Felton. "As sweet as honey, as warm as the sun..."

"And thou – " he said, turning to squint down at the playbook in his hands. "Thou, my darling Hannah, told me of thine heart, of the ways in which – "

Elizabeth's body went limp, falling back against the chaise in a cold faint.

I leapt dramatically to my feet. "Lizzie?" I gasped. "Lizzie, can you hear me?"

I gave her a gentle shake, but she did not move.

All the voices apart from Miss Colette's went silent as I laid my hand upon Elizabeth's forehead. "No fever..." I declared.

"What happened?" asked Mr. Langley, who appeared at my elbow just a moment later.

"I do not know," I said. "We were just sitting here, and she – she fainted."

"She was saying that she was feeling a bit dizzy," Miss Carter said, abandoning her book to come over to us.

Felton pushed past Miss Colette to see me, worry knitting his brows together. "She fainted?" he asked, removing his jacket. He rolled it up into a ball and gently lifted Elizabeth's head, tucking it underneath. "She was complaining of feeling unwell?"

Sir Livingston leaned over the side of the chaise, waving a thin book to fan Elizabeth's face, causing her hair to flutter.

"I shall go and fetch some cold towels from our room," I said. "And her medicine."

"Medicine?" Felton asked. "Has this happened before?"

"She has always been prone to fainting easily," I said. "Ever since she was a child. I am terribly sorry – "

"You need not apologize," Mr. Browne said. "How could you possibly have known this would happen?"

"I believe it was all the excitement," I said.

"Well, go fetch what she needs," Miss Carter said. "I assure you, we shall keep an eye on her while you are gone."

I looked over at Felton whose expression had turned to one of worry; it was a face that Miles had worn when he had learned that Joan had gone missing. It was the sole reason I could know for certain that our host was taking this all quite seriously. "As Miss Carter said," he said. "She shall be in good hands. I will be certain to send for some cool water for when she wakes, and see if Mr. Henry can scrounge up some fragrant salts to help bring her round."

"All right," I said. "I will not be long..." Then I frowned. "Oh, but her medicine. I do hope I shall be able to find it."

"Do not delay any longer," Mr. Browne said, shooing me on. "Off you go, then!"

I turned and scurried from the room, leaving the

rest of the guests murmuring and fussing over Elizabeth's still form.

As soon as my foot hit the first step, a smile spread across my face.

Elizabeth, you genius! I thought, racing up the stairs, spurred on by the very reality that my time was limited, and perhaps not entirely guaranteed.

She would have certainly heard every word, every concern from all of the guests gathering around her. Her acting outshone that of anything Miss Colette and Felton Beechwood had done, lying there as still as she was. We had agreed that she would remain still for a few moments, and then come to, seeming confused and bewildered. This would be followed by a moment of sheer embarrassment wherein she would burst into tears. We assumed that either Miss Carter or Sir Livingston would try to comfort her. After that, she would ask for something to drink, and share how she had been feeling with them all, explaining her supposed illness.

By that time, I hoped I would be back with a pack of mints that she had previously tucked into a tin and given to me. They would look enough like medicine that no one should question them. I patted my pocket to ensure the tin was still there. It was.

I bypassed our guest room and the others, making my way to the staircase leading to the next floor. My heart thundered in my ears. My excuse of being lost would only work with a servant who had not seen me too many times, and I would have to try and seem as worried as I had downstairs.

Even if all I accomplished was to find a place that looked promising, I could always come back later this evening when everyone else was asleep...if everyone did not insist that Elizabeth and I leave early for the sake of her health. A cold chill swept over me. We had not considered that possibility.

I reached the top floor, and began to peer into rooms. Thankfully, I had managed not to meet anyone on the stairs or the landing, and that gave me plenty of chances to look around. I found a second library, a handful of bedrooms so plain they must have belonged to some of the staff, and a number of storerooms. No studies, no obvious places that Felton may have been alluding to.

I stood inside the doorway of one of the darkened storerooms, tapping my finger frantically against my cheek, as if it might dislodge any ideas. I had to hurry. My time was quickly running out.

This whole trip could end up being entirely for naught, I thought miserably. *What if we came all this distance, and I worked my way into the very heart of the home of Sophia's killer, only to fail at discovering a single piece of evidence?*

I shook my head. It would be far too easy to give in to desperation. I needed to focus.

Where could I look? There had to be something.

The room I had passed earlier at the end of the hall had been yet another storeroom, but it had been filled with boxes, crates, and covered furniture. I assumed they were being prepared to go to Miles' home in London whenever Felton meant to move in. I had bypassed it entirely, thinking that Felton would not have hidden something involving framing Miles with the intent to send it back to Miles' house.

But then again...

I made my way back to the room, fear humming in my ears as I knew how little time I had left. When I stepped inside, the thought struck me that maybe it *would* make sense for him to pack up some incriminating evidence to send there. Could he not then just blame it further on Miles? Not only would it be hidden until he moved, but if he had left it out, it would be more likely for someone to find it here, at his estate.

It might have been a bit of a stretch, but I had to check.

I stepped inside, meandering among the boxes. Lifting the lids, I found dishware, linens, clothing... nothing of use.

I turned back to the door as I heard a clock chime downstairs somewhere. I had been gone for almost ten minutes, and they would surely be wondering where I had gotten off to. A glint of gold, gleaming in the beam of the hall light peeking into the room, caught my eye.

I made my way to it, and found a simple leather brief-case with the initials *FB* stitched in gold thread on the front.

My heart pounded. It was unlocked, too.

My fingers trembled as I flipped open the top.

15

I
f I had hoped for a note at the very top reading *I killed Sophia! Signed, Felton Beechwood,* I was highly disappointed.

It contained what I might have expected from a briefcase; papers, old pens, some thin, narrow books without any titles or names upon them or their spines. I huffed in annoyance, meaning to shove the thing away...when I realized that the uninteresting covers might have been on purpose. I reached for the top one, covered in a deep leafy green. Flipping it open, I noticed a spidery script within, uneven and blotchy in places. *Handwritten, no doubt, and apparently rather hasty,* I thought. I glanced at the top of the page, noticing a date.

September 13, 1925

A journal, perhaps?

A quick scan through the paragraphs did not give me a great deal of confidence in its writer, apart from the hope they belonged to the same owner of the initials. *If this does belong to Felton, and these are his journals...* I thought.

I set the first journal aside, and selected the next, opening it up.

July 28, 1928

My heart skipped. That was just last summer! That may well mean...

I grabbed for the third journal, and found to my great delight that it began in 1929, the year that Sophia met her end.

I passed through the entries looking only for two names; Nicholas, and Sophia. I managed to find them rather quickly, and it amazed me how fond the entries seemed. No hatred, no nastiness...

What if we were wrong? What if –

But then I paused my worrying, staring down at the page.

The entry was messy, scratched out in many places, and carried on for several pages. It was difficult to put the string of thoughts together, but there was no doubt; in it, he admitted to killing Sophia. He went on to write about his financial worries, attempting to justify his actions as being born of a necessity to obtain the inheritance that would relieve his debts.

The entry as a whole was not quite what I had

expected, filled with regret and fear, not boasting as Miles had once expected.

I wasted no time. I shoved the others back into the briefcase, pocketed the one small volume I needed, and moved to lay the briefcase precisely where I had found it in the shadows...when I heard a shifting of clothing behind me.

I froze, half bent over the briefcase. I hoped wildly that it was only one of the servants who had caught me. My mind raced to come up with some believable story –

But a sense of dread deep inside told me it was not a servant...but Felton. It had to be. Who else would have known precisely where to find me?

I stood, turning around, and my gaze fell upon Felton in the doorway. He did not look particularly angry, but he certainly had lost the expression of worry that he had worn earlier when I had fled the drawing room.

"I suppose there is no point in telling you that your cousin is now awake and quite recovered," he said. "As I assume you already know that."

My face colored. I had to find a way out of this, and quickly. Perhaps he did not see me pocket the book?

"I hope you do not think me an ungracious host if I ask why you would create such a ruse in order to go through my belongings?" he asked. "Snooping through a private journal, no less."

*So much for that...*I thought.

"What I cannot figure out..." he said, leaning against the doorframe, entirely blocking my exit. "Is what you are playing at?"

I could still get out of this. I could still find a way to get home without answering him.

"Because..." he continued, sliding his hands gracefully into the pockets of his trousers. "I would hate to imagine that you are snooping for something in particular... Now, what could that possibly be?"

My heart thundered in my ears. He was toying with me.

"I have thought you were acting strangely all along," he went on. "Something seemed different about you from the beginning. You have been asking about the house, looking around, your gaze constantly sweeping through the rooms, as if searching for something." He shook his head. "So I began watching you, sensing that your intentions were anything but honest."

"That shows how little you know," I said automatically, glaring at him. "Compared to what you've done, I am not the one whose honesty should be questioned –
"

I stumbled over my words, as I realized what I had done.

Felton's face darkened and he moved further into the room, kicking the door closed behind him.

"Who put you up to this?" he asked, his voice stony. "Who figured it all out?"

"I – " I said, backing up against one of the boxes, the corner jabbing me squarely in the back. I swallowed hard. How could I possibly get out of this now?"

"There is only one person it could be," he growled, stalking closer to me. "It would have to be Nicholas. He should be *dead*."

I could nearly feel the heat emanating from him, the hatred, and the seething anger.

I had no choice. In such a confined space, I could not let him come any closer. He could easily overpower me, and given that everyone else was so far away –

I reached behind me, into the waistband of my skirt, retrieving a cold, heavy object that had been concealed by the length of my bulky cardigan. Withdrawing the narrow pistol I had hoped I would not need, I pointed it squarely at Felton.

I was grateful now for the fear or premonition that had caused me to steal Miles' gun from his room before we had left Elizabeth's house. That same instinct had made me remove the weapon from my luggage and stow it upon my person during my last visit to my own room here.

"I feared it would come to this..." I said, doing my best to keep my hands steady. With any luck, the mere appearance that I was prepared to defend myself would deter him. I didn't know if I could actually shoot if the time came to try.

"That belonged to Nicholas..." Felton breathed, staring at the pistol.

I supposed it made sense that he recognized the gun, since it had once been in his own possession.

"How did you – how could you possibly have come by it?" he asked.

I said nothing. He did not need to know what I did.

He gazed at me, and then at the pistol again. "You know him. You are *working* with him. You must be!"

He lashed out with his leg, giving the crate beside me a mighty kick. I moved quickly out of the way as his foot collided with it, the wooden boards splintering with the force.

"What a coward my cousin is!" he snarled. "He must have known that the only way he could sneak in here would be to have a woman do his snooping for him!" In frustration, he knotted his hands in his sandy hair that looked so like Miles'. "I should have killed him too when I had the chance!"

Before I could think to react, he lunged suddenly at me, reaching out with groping fingers.

I ducked away, but not fast enough to prevent him from grabbing hold of the pistol and tearing it from my grasp. He shoved me with one hand, and I staggered back, before falling against the dirty floor.

He turned the pistol over in his hands, gazing at it

from all angles. "I remember this pistol..." he said. "And what a shame it will be to have to take another life with it."

He lowered it to me, pointing it squarely at my head, as I sat frozen with shock.

"Remember the woman I said that you reminded me of?" he asked, a smirk dancing across his face. "She is the other one who met her fate at the end of this same gun."

"I know..." I said, my brain kicking into action again. In the absence of any other plan, all I could do was to keep him talking. Slowly, my eyes on the gun, I got back to my feet. "You mean the wife of Mi – of Nicholas. Her name was Sophia."

His eyebrows raised. "So, you are informed," he said.

"You killed her so you could take his inheritance," I said.

He said nothing, but I saw a flash of fear in his gaze. I realized with a start that he was feigning confidence and attempting to appear indifferent. But I could still hear in my mind the conflicted thoughts I had read in the diary.

"You went to great lengths to trick her to come out with you, killing her in a public space so that others might see you and mistake you for your cousin," I said. "Everyone blames Nicholas for it, so you somehow got away with it."

"Clearly I did not cover my tracks well enough," he said, and without further warning, he pulled the trigger.

I dropped to the floor the instant before the gun went off. I had seen the decision in his face the moment he reached it, had seen that he had fully made up his mind what he must do.

The bullet shot through the air, zinging through a shuttered window behind me, and shattering the glass as it went. The echo of the gun's explosion seemed to fill the small room.

*Everyone in the house will have heard that...*I thought. It was only a matter of time before someone got up here to see what was happening.

Perhaps my enemy thought the same, for he shook his head sharply.

"No matter," he said, coming toward me. He scooped me into the air by the collar of my blouse, choking me as he dragged me across to the broken window. I gasped for air, as I struggled against his hold.

I didn't have to think twice about what his intentions were. He meant to throw me out, perhaps shooting me first for good measure. I could not imagine what excuse he would give to the world. Perhaps a claim that I had attacked him for some reason and he had acted in self-defense? Or that I had turned the gun on myself? One thing I knew. He had been clever enough to get away with murder once before. There was a chance that, one way or another, he would cover his tracks again this time. And without me, how could Miles prove his innocence?

I only had one chance to stop him. He was too strong for me to wrestle out of his grip; I tried, but he held fast as if I were no stronger than a child.

My frantically searching hand swept across the floor as we drew nearer to the shattered glass, and I snatched up one of the broken shards. Without waiting for him to hoist me up, I immediately drove the shard deep into the soft flesh of the underside of his calf.

Shrieking in pain and surprise, he dropped me at once. I slammed against the ground, some of the loose glass slicing through my sleeve. I winced as I tried to push myself up onto my hands, looking up just in time to see Felton teeter near the window, off balance. He tried to reach down to pull the shard out, but he lost his footing on the floor, which was already slick with the blood gushing from his wound. He slipped and fell toward the opening of the broken window...

And plunged the four stories down to the lawn below.

16

"Sylvia…"

At the familiar voice, I looked up from the little nest I had been placed within. Blankets wrapped around my shoulders, teacups continually filled and pressed into my hands, a chair beside the fire… It was the recipe for relaxing, though not what I had expected to be doing at the end of such a day.

Miles strode into the room, Elizabeth and Mr. Walton close behind.

I moved to stand, as Miles hurried to my side. "No, please, do not get up," he said. He knelt down in front of me, anxiously examining my face, as if for signs of injury. "I will never forgive myself for leaving you as I did," he said. "And all for a *lead* that turned out to be nothing."

"How did you know we were here?" I asked, bewildered.

"I'm afraid I am to blame," Elizabeth said, strolling over to me. "The last time I telephoned home, Miles overheard Peter's end of our conversation. It was enough for him to realize what was going on. He demanded Peter tell him the details, and then they apparently headed this way immediately."

"And yet, I am too late, arriving only after the danger is past," Miles said with a frown.

"Well, if you had been any earlier, you would have jeopardized the whole affair," I pointed out. "Coming right to your cousin's house would have been reckless."

"I would not care, if it meant saving you," he said. "If I had known what you were planning – "

"I know, you never would have let me come in the first place," I said.

His frown deepened. "Sylvia, what would I have done if you had been hurt? What would I have done if he had succeeded?"

I glanced at Elizabeth, who turned away, sheepish. It seemed that after meeting him at the front door, she had filled him in on the remaining details of my encounter with Felton a few hours beforehand.

"My deepest regret is that I was not here sooner..." he said. "I should have confronted him on my own, not wasted time in the city, hoping to find my break. It was foolishness, and could have gotten you killed."

His expression softened as he covered one of my hands with his own.

"Perhaps...we should give them a few moments?" Mr. Walton said.

"Oh, yes, of course, of course," Elizabeth said. "We shall go speak with Mr. Henry. If the police are still here, they may have more questions for you."

"Let them come in if they do," I said wearily. I hoped it would not be necessary, however, as I had already spoken with the authorities upon their arrival earlier, after instructing Mr. Henry to summon them. Like the other servants, and most of the guests, the butler seemed to be handling the shocking turn of events with a surprising degree of calm.

Elizabeth and Mr. Walton left the room, leaving Miles and I in there together.

"I'm sorry..." I said, after a few moments. "About Felton."

Miles took the chair beside mine, but his expression became blank. "I am not," he said. "He reaped what he sowed, didn't he?"

"I suppose..." I said, turning the sleeve of my cardigan over, noticing some of the blood that had seeped through two layers of fabric to stain both my cardigan and the blouse beneath it. The blood wasn't my own, but had come from Felton's leg when I had stabbed him.

"Here. You should read this," I said. I pulled the

journal from the side table where I had put it for safe keeping. "Your proof, as promised."

Miles' eyes widened, and he took it.

I gave him some time to read through it, watching his face change as he read the entries. I caught glimpses of grief, nostalgia, and anger. Eventually, he closed it, laying a hand over it gently, slowly.

"Well?" I asked.

"It brought back a great many memories..." he said. "But you are right. It is the proof we are looking for. Irrefutable, really, between your testimony of what he told you and this journal in his handwriting."

"How do you feel?" I asked. "You can have your name cleared before the end of the day, if you so choose."

"A few months ago, that might have been all I would have wanted..." he said, looking over at me. "But my priorities have changed."

I tilted my head. What did he mean?

"I have made up my mind about something," he said. "This trip to London has solidified it for me."

"Well? Are you going to share what it is?" I asked.

He smiled, his eyes dancing. "I never thought I could find someone I cared for as much as I loved Sophia. When I lost her, my world fell apart."

I became very still. I didn't quite know what to expect, but I had a suspicion I knew where he was going with this.

"At the time, I thought only of revenge, but now I realize revenge would have made me no better than Felton was. It wouldn't have restored my happiness. Not really. It wasn't until I met you, Sylvia, that I realized there might be hope of something better to live for. I can no longer deny the fact that I have fallen in love with you. Deeply, truly. We have been through far too much for it to be anything else."

"Miles..." I said, hardly knowing what to say.

He smiled at me. "I believe it is past time that you started to call me by my real name."

"You mean *Nicholas*?"

He chuckled. "It sounds awfully strange coming from you..." he said. "Though I suppose I had best get used to it." He regarded me patiently. "And what do you say? If you have no answer for me, then I will be content to wait for – "

"No," I said, then quickly recovered. "What I mean to say is that I do know. I have known for some time. It seems that everyone has known it but me. You have had my heart for a long time, and to try and deny it any longer would just be foolish. I have never loved someone the way that I love you...nor do I think I ever could, given what we have endured."

A smile, warm and genuine, spread across his face. "Then, Miss Sylvia Shipman, now that I can be worthy of you with a clear name and conscience...would you do me the honor of marrying me?"

I sat there, in that quiet drawing room in the house of a man who had utterly ruined his life, listening to words that might change mine forever.

Marriage to Miles...

It would be a lie to say that the thought had not occurred to me, at least since our arrival in London. It had probably been playing at the back of my mind even longer than I knew...which made my answer easy to arrive at.

"On one condition..." I said, smirking at him. "That you will never try to tackle another mystery without me again."

He burst out laughing. "You have my word..." he said. "And my heart. For all of my days."

Continue the mysterious adventures of Sylvia Shipman in "Murder With Mirth: A Sylvia Shipman Murder Mystery Book 7."

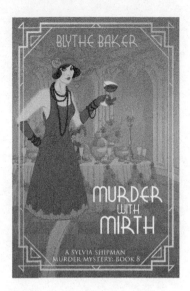

ABOUT THE AUTHOR

Blythe Baker is the lead writer behind several popular historical and paranormal mystery series. When Blythe isn't buried under clues, suspects, and motives, she's acting as chauffeur to her children and head groomer to her household of beloved pets. She enjoys walking her dogs, lounging in her backyard hammock, and fiddling with graphic design. She also likes binge-watching mystery shows on TV. To learn more about Blythe, visit her website and sign up for her newsletter at www.blythebaker.com

Made in the USA
Las Vegas, NV
01 November 2023

80086805R00132